WHEN A MAN'S SINGLE

"YOU ARE CRYING," HE SAID

WHEN A MAN'S SINGLE
A TALE OF LITERARY LIFE

BY

J. M. BARRIE

WILDSIDE PRESS

www.wildsidepress.com

TO

W. ROBERTSON NICOLL, M. A.

INTRODUCTION*

"WHEN a Man's Single" was first published from week to week in the *British Weekly;* it began to appear there before more than two chapters of it were written; soon I was only one chapter ahead, and after that, I think, I never increased the distance between us though I could feel its breath on my neck. This perhaps accounts for the curiously inappropriate title; until he was married (from which point I cannot answer for him) Rob Angus never "lived at his ease." I expect that when I started Rob I meant him to have a less strenuous time, but he fell in love, and once they fall in love there is no saying what your heroes will do. By that time the book was christened and had got used to its name.

Titles, however, are a small matter; the chief objection to this form of publication is that it prevents the spontaneous development of your tale. There are writers who can plan out their story beforehand as clearly as though it were a railway journey, and adhere throughout to their original design — they draw up what playwrights call a

* Copyright, 1896, by Charles Scribner's Sons.
Written for the first collected uniform edition.

INTRODUCTION

scenario — but I was never one of those. I spend a great deal of time indeed in looking for the best road in the map and mark it with red ink, but at the first bypath off my characters go. "Come back," I cry, "you are off the road." "We prefer this way," they reply. I try bullying. "You are only people in a book," I shout, "and it is my book, and I can do what I like with you, so come back!" But they seldom come, and it ends with my plodding after them. Unless I am the one to yield, they and I do not become good friends, which is fatal to the book, but, if they do something not in the plan, it often necessitates altera- tions in the preceding chapters, and such alterations cannot be made when these chapters are already in print. Thus, oftener than was wise, I dragged Rob Angus and his friends back to the main road, and when I let them stray it was at a cost. These are some reasons why the book is so disjointed. It is a method of publication I hope never to adopt again.

CONTENTS

WHEN A MAN'S SINGLE

CHAPTER I

ROB ANGUS IS NOT A FREE MAN

ONE still Saturday afternoon some years ago a child pulled herself through a small window into a kitchen in the kirk-wynd of Thrums. She came from the old graveyard, whose only outlet, when the parish church gate is locked, is the windows of the wynd houses that hoop it round. Squatting on a three-legged stool she gazed wistfully at a letter on the chimney-piece, and then, tripping to the door, looked up and down the wynd.

Snecky Hobart, the bellman, hobbled past, and, though Davy was only four years old, she knew that as he had put on his blue top-coat he expected the evening to be fine. Tammas McQuhatty, the farmer of T'nowhead, met him at the corner, and they came to a standstill to say, "She's hard, Sneck," and "She is so, T'nowhead," referring to

WHEN A MAN'S SINGLE

the weather. Observing that they had stopped they moved on again.

Women and children and a few men squeezed through their windows into the kirk-yard, the women to knit stockings on fallen tombstones, and the men to dander pleasantly from grave to grave reading the inscriptions. All the men were well up in years, for though, with the Auld Lichts, the Sabbath began to come on at six o'clock on Saturday evening, the young men were now washing themselves cautiously in tin basins before going into the square to talk about women.

The clatter of more than one loom could still have been heard by Davy had not her ears been too accustomed to the sound to notice it. In the adjoining house Bell Mealmaker was peppering her newly-washed floor with sand, while her lodger, Hender Robb, with a rusty razor in his hand, looked for his chin in a tiny glass that was peeling on the wall. Jinny Tosh had got her husband, Aundra Lunan, who always spoke of her as She, ready, so as to speak, for church eighteen hours too soon, and Aundra sat stiffly at the fire, putting his feet on the ribs every minute, to draw them back with a scared look at Her as he remembered that he had on his blacks. In a bandbox beneath the bed was his silk hat, which had been knocked down to him at Jamie Ramsay's roup, and Jinny had already put his red handkerchief, which was also a

2

pictorial history of Scotland, into a pocket of his coat-tails, with a corner hanging gracefully out. Her puckered lips signified that, however much her man might desire to do so, he was not to carry his handkerchief to church in his hat, where no one could see it. On working days Aundra held his own, but at six o'clock on Saturday nights he passed into Her hands.

Across the wynd, in which a few hens wandered, Pete Todd was supping in his shirt-sleeves. His blacks lay ready for him in the coffin-bed, and Pete, glancing at them at intervals, supped as slowly as he could. In one hand he held a saucer, and in the other a chunk of bread, and they were as far apart as Pete's outstretched arms could put them. His chair was a yard from the table, on which, by careful balancing, he rested a shoeless foot, and his face was twisted to the side. Every time Easie Whamond, his wife, passed him she took the saucer from his hand, remarking that when a genteel man sat down to tea he did not turn his back on the table. Pete took this stolidly, like one who had long given up trying to understand the tantrums of women, and who felt that, as a lord of creation, he could afford to let it pass.

Davy sat on her three-legged stool keeping guard over her uncle Rob the saw-miller's letter, and longing for him to come. She screwed up her eyebrows as she had seen him do when he read a

WHEN A MAN'S SINGLE

letter, and she felt that it would be nice if every one would come and look at her taking care of it. After a time she climbed up on her stool and stretched her dimpled arms toward the mantel-piece. From a string suspended across this, socks and stockings hung drying at the fire, and clutch-ing one of them Davy drew herself nearer. With a chuckle, quickly suppressed, lest it should bring in Kitty Wilkie, who ought to have been watch-ing her instead of wandering down the wynd to see who was to have salt fish for supper, the child clutched the letter triumphantly, and, toddling to the door, slipped out of the house.

For a moment Davy faltered at the mouth of the wynd. There was no one there to whom she could show the letter. A bright thought entered her head, and immediately a dimple opened on her face and swallowed all the puckers. Rob had gone to the Whunny muir for wood, and she would take the letter to him. Then when Rob saw her he would look all around him, and if there was no one there to take note he would lift her to his shoulder, when they could read the letter together.

Davy ran out of the wynd into the square, think-ing she heard Kitty's Sabbath voice, which re-minded the child of the little squeaking saw that Rob used for soft wood. On week-days Kitty's voice was the big saw that pulled and rasped, and

Mag Wilkie shivered at it. Except to her husband Mag spoke with her teeth closed, so politely that no one knew what she said.

Davy stumbled up the steep brae down which men are blown in winter to their work, until she reached the rim of the hollow in which Thrums lies. Here the road stops short, as if frightened to cross the common of whin that bars the way to the north. On this common there are many cart-tracks over bumpy sward and slippery roots, that might be the ribs of the earth showing, and Davy, with a dazed look in her eyes, ran down one of them, the whins catching her frock to stop her, and then letting go, as if, after all, one child more or less in the world was nothing to them.

By and by she found herself on another road, along which Rob had trudged earlier in the day with a saw on his shoulder, but he had gone east, and the child's face was turned westward. It is a muddy road even in summer, and those who use it frequently get into the habit of lifting their legs high as they walk, like men picking their way through beds of rotting leaves. The light had faded from her baby face now, but her mouth was firm-set, and her bewildered eyes were fixed straight ahead.

The last person to see Davy was Tammas Haggart, who, with his waistcoat buttoned over his jacket, and garters of yarn round his trousers,

WHEN A MAN'S SINGLE

was slowly breaking stones, though the road swallowed them quicker than he could ✻ed it. Tammas heard the child approaching, for his hearing
had become very acute, owing to his practice when
at home of listening through the floor to what the
folks below were saying, and of sometimes joining
in. He leant on his hammer and watched her
trot past.

The strength went gradually from Tammas's old
arms, and again resting on his hammer he removed
his spectacles and wiped them on his waistcoat.
He took a comprehensive glance around at the
fields, as if he now had an opportunity of seeing
them for the first time during his sixty years' pil-
grimage in these parts, and his eyes wandered
aimlessly from the sombre firs and laughing beeches
to the white farms that dot the strath. In the fore-
ground two lazy colts surveyed him critically
across a dyke. To the north the frowning Whunny
hill had a white scarf round its neck.

Something troubled Tammas. It was the vision
of a child in a draggled pinafore, and stepping into
the middle of the road he looked down it in the
direction in which Davy had passed.

" Chirsty Angus's lassieky," he murmured.

Tammas sat down cautiously on the dyke and
untied the red handkerchief that contained the
remnants of his dinner. When he had smacked
his lips over his flagon of cold kail, and seen the

last of his crumbling oatmeal and cheese, his un-
easiness retui ..d, and he again looked down the
road.

" I maun turn the bairn," was his reflection.

It was now, however, half an hour since Davy
had passed Tammas Haggart's cairn.

To Haggart, pondering between the strokes of
his hammer, came a mole-catcher, who climbed the
dyke and sat down beside him.

" Ay, ay," said the new-comer; to which Tammas replied abstractedly —

" Jamie."

" Hae ye seen Davy Dundas ? " the stone-breaker
asked, after the pause that followed this conversation.

The mole-catcher stared heavily at his corduroys.

" I dinna ken him," he said, at last, " but I hae
seen naebody this twa 'oors."

" It's no a him, it's a her. Ye canna hae been a
winter here without kennin' Rob Angus."

" Ay, the saw-miller. He was i' the wud the
day. I saw his cart gae hame. Ou, in coorse I
ken Rob. He's an amazin' crittur."

Tammas broke another stone as carefully as if
it were a nut.

" I dinna deny," he said, " but what Rob's a
turiosity. So was his faither afore 'im."

" I've heard auld Rob was a queer body," said

7

Jamie, adding incredulously, " they say he shaved twice i' the week an' wore a clean dicky ilka day."

" No what ye wad say ilka day, but oftener than was called for. Rob wasna naturally ostentatious; na, it was the wife 'at insist on't. Nanny was a terrible tid for cleanness. Ay, an' it's a guid thing in moderation, but she juist overdid it; yes, she overdid it. Man, it had sic a haud on her 'at even on her deathbed they had to bring a basin to her to wash her hands in."

" Ay, ay? When there was sic a pride in her I wonder she didna lat young Rob to the college, an' him sae keen on't."

" Ou, he was gaen, but ye see auld Rob got gey dottle after Nanny's death, an' so young Rob stuck to the saw-mill. It's curious hoo a body misses his wife when she's gone. Ay, it's like the clock stoppin'."

" Weel, Rob's no gettin' to the college hasna made 'im humble."

" Ye dinna like Rob? "

" Hoo did ye find that oot?" asked Jamie, a little taken aback. " Man, Tammas," he added, admiringly, " ye're michty quick i' the uptak."

Tammas handed his snuff-mull to the mole-catcher, and then helped himself.

" I daursay, I daursay," he said, thoughtfully. " I've naething to say agin the saw-miller," continued Jamie, after thinking it out, " but there's

ROB ANGUS IS NOT A FREE MAN

something in's face 'at's no sociable. He looks as
if he was takkin' ye aff in's inside."

"Ay, auld Rob was a sarcestic stock too. It
rins i' the blood."

"I prefer a mair common kind o' man, bein' o'
the common kind mysel'."

"Ay, there's naething sarcestic about you,
Jamie," admitted the stone-breaker.

"I'm an ord'nar man, Tammas."

"Ye are, Jamie, ye are."

"Maybe no sae oncommon ord'nar either."

"Midlin' ord'nar, midlin' ord'nar."

"I'm thinkin' ye're braw an' sarcestic yersel,
Tammas?"

"I'd aye that repootation, Jeames. Am no an
everyday sarcesticist, but juist noos an' nans.
There was ae time I was speakin' tae Easie
Webster, an' I said a terrible sarcestic thing. Ay,
I dinna mind what it was, but it was michty sar-
cestic."

"It's a gift," said the mole-catcher.

"A gift it is," said Tammas.

The stone-breaker took his flagon to a spring
near at hand, and rinsed it out. Several times
while pulling it up and down the little pool an
uneasy expression crossed his face as he remembered something about a child, but in washing his
hands, using sand for soap, Davy slipped his
memory, and he returned cheerfully to the cairn.

9

Here Jamie was wagging his head from side to side like a man who had caught himself thinking.

" I'll warrant, Tammas," he said, " ye cudna tell's what set's on to speak aboot Rob Angus ? "

" Na, it's a thing as has often puzzled me hoo we select wan topic mair than anither. I suppose it's like shootin'; ye juist blaze awa' at the first bird 'at rises."

" Ye was sayin', had I seen a lass wi' a lad's name. That began it, I'm thinkin'."

" A lass wi' a lad's name ? Ay, noo, that's on-common. But mebbe ye mean Davy Dundas ? "

" That's the name."

Tammas paused in the act of buttoning his trouser pocket.

" Did ye say ye'd seen Davy ? " he asked.

" Na, it was you as said 'at ye had seen her."

" Ay, ay, Jamie, ye're richt. Man, I fully meant to turn the bairn, but she ran by at sic a steek 'at there was nae stoppin' her. Rob'll mak an awfu' ring-ding if onything comes ower Davy."

" Is't the litlin 'ats aye wi' Rob ? "

" Ay, it's Chirsty Angus's bairn, her 'at was Rob's sister. A' her fowk's deid but Rob."

" I've seen them i' the saw-mill thegither. It didna strick me 'at Rob cared muckle for the crittury."

" Ou, Rob's a reserved stock, but he's michty fond o' her when naebody's lookin'. It doesna do, ye ken, to lat on afore company at ye've a kind o' regaird for yere ain fowk. Na, it's lowerin'. But if it wasna afore your time, ye'd seen the cradle i' the saw-mill."

" I never saw ony cradle, Tammas."

" Weel, it was unco' ingenious o' Rob. The bairn's father an' mither was baith gone when Davy was nae age, an' auld Rob passed awa' sune efter. Rob had it all arranged to ging to the college — ay, he'd been workin' far on into the nicht the hale year to save up siller to keep 'imsel at Edinbory, but ye see he promised Chirsty to look after Davy an' no' send her to the parish. He took her to the saw-mill an' brocht her up 'imsel. It was a terrible disappointment to Rob, his mind bein' bent on becomin' a great leeterary genius, but he's been michty guid to the bairn. Ay, she's an extror'nar takkin' dawty, Davy, an' though I wudna like it kent, I've a fell notion o' her mysel. I mind ance gaen in to Rob's, an', wud ye believe, there was the bit lassieky sitting in the airmchair wi' ane o' Rob's books open on her knees, an' her pertendin' to be readin' oot in't to Rob. The tiddy had watched him readin', ye unerstan', an', man, she was mimickin' 'im to the life. There's nae accountin' for thae things, but ondootedly it was attractive."

· " But what aboot a cradle ? "

" Ou, as I was sayin', Rob didna like to lat the bairn oot o' his sicht, so he made a queer cradle

11

'imsel, an' put it ower the burn. Ye'll mind the burn rins through the saw-mill? Ay, weel, Davy's cradle was put across't wi' the paddles sae arranged 'at the watter rocked the cradle. Man, the burn was juist like a mither to Davy, for no' only did it rock her to sleep, but it sang to the bairn the hale time."

" That was an ingenious contrivance, Tammas; but it was juist like Rob Angus's ind'pendence. The crittur aye perseests in doin' a'thing for 'imsel. I mind ae day seein' Cree Deuchars puttin' in a window into the saw-mill hoose, an' Rob's fingers was fair itchin' to do't quick 'imsel; ye ken Cree's fell slow? 'See haud o' the potty,' cries Rob, an' losh, he had the window in afore Cree cud hae cut the glass. Ay, ye canna deny but what Rob's fearfu' independent."

" So was his faither. I call to mind auld Rob an' the minister haen a termendous debate aboot justification by faith, an' says Rob i' the tail o' the day, gettin' passionate-like, 'I tell ye flat, Mester Byars,' he says, 'if I dinna ging to heaven in my ain wy, I dinna ging ava!'"

" Losh, losh! he wudna hae said that, though, to oor minister; na, he wudna hae daured."

" Ye're a U. P., Jamie?" asked the stone-breaker.

" I was born U. P.," replied the mole-catcher, firmly, "an' U. P. I'll die."

ROB ANGUS IS NOT A FREE MAN

"I say naething agin yer releegion," replied Tammas, a little contemptuously, "but to compare yer minister to oors is a haver. Man, when Mester Byars was oor minister, Sanders Dobie, the wricht, had a standin' engagement to mend the poopit ilka month."

"We'll no' speak o' releegion, Tammas, or we'll be quarrellin'. Ye micht tell's, though, hoo they cam to gie a lassieky sic a man's name as Davy."

"It was an accident at the christenin'. Ye see, Hendry Dundas an' Chirsty was both vary young, an' when the bairn was born they were shy-like aboot makkin' the affair public; ay, Hendry cud hardly tak courage to tell the minister. When he was haddin' up the bit tid in the kirk to be baptized he was remarkable egitated. Weel, the minister — it was Mester Dishart — somehoo had a notion 'at the litlin was a laddie, an' when he reads the name on the paper, 'Margaret Dundas,' he looks at Hendry wi' the bairny in's airms, an' says he, stern-like, 'The child's a boy, is he not?'"

"Sal, that was a predeecament for Hendry."

"Ay, an' Hendry was confused, as a man often is wi' his first; so says he, all trem'lin', 'Yes, Mr. Dishart.' 'Then,' says the minister, 'I cannot christen him Margaret, so I will call him David.' An' Davit the litlin was baptized, sure eneuch."

"The mither wud be in a michty wy at that?"

13

WHEN A MAN'S SINGLE

"She was so, but as Hendry said, when she challenged him on the subject, says Hendry, 'I dauredna conterdick the minister.'"

Haggart's work being now over for the day, he sat down beside Jamie to await some other stone-breakers who generally caught him up on their way home. Strange figures began to emerge from the woods, a dumb man with a barrowful of roots for firewood, several women in men's coats, one smoking a cutty-pipe. A farm-labourer pulled his heavy legs in their rustling corduroys alongside a field of swedes, a ragged potato bogle brandished its arms in a sudden puff of wind. Several men and women reached Haggart's cairn about the same time, and said, "It is so," or "ay, ay," to him, according as they were loquacious or merely polite.

" We was speakin' aboot matermony," the mole-catcher remarked, as the back-bent little party straggled toward Thrums.

"It's a caution," murmured the farm-labourer, who had heard the observation from the other side of the dyke. "Ay, ye may say so," he added, thoughtfully addressing himself.

With the mole-catcher's companions, however, the talk passed into another rut. Nevertheless Haggart was thinking matrimony over, and by and by he saw his way to a joke, for one of the other stone-breakers had recently married a very

14

small woman, and in Thrums, where women have to work, the far-seeing men prefer their wives big.

"Ye drew a sma' prize yersel, Sam'l," said Tammas, with the gleam in his eye which showed that he was now in sarcastic fettle.

"Ay," said the mole-catcher, "Sam'l's Kitty is sma'. I suppose Sam'l thocht it wud be prudent-like to begin in a modest wy."

"If Kitty hadna haen sae sma' hands," said another stone-breaker, "I wud hae haen a bid for her mysel."

The women smiled; they had very large hands.

"They say," said the youngest of them, who had a load of firewood on her back, "'at there's places whaur little hands is thocht muckle o'."

There was an incredulous laugh at this.

"I wudna wonder, though," said the mole-catcher, who had travelled; "there's some michty queer ideas i' the big toons."

"Ye'd better ging to the big toons, then, Sam'l," suggested the merciless Tammas.

Sam'l woke up.

"Kitty's sma'," he said, with a chuckle, "but she's an auld tid."

"What made ye think o' speirin' her, Sam'l?"

"I cudna say for sartin," answered Sam'l, reflectively. "I had nae intention o't till I saw Pete Proctor after her, an' syne, thinks I, I'll hae her.

Ay, ye micht say as Pete was the instrument o'
Providence in that case."

" Man, man," murmured Jamie, who knew Pete,
" Providence sometimes maks use o' strange instru-
ments."

" Ye was lang in gettin' a man yersel, Jinny,"
said Tammas to an elderly woman.

" Fower an' forty year," replied Jinny. ' It was
like a stockin', lang i' the futin', but turned at
last."

" Lassies nooadays," said the old woman who
smoked, " is partikler by what they used to be. I
mind when Jeames Gowrie speired me : ' Ye wud
raither hae Davit Curly, I ken,' he says. ' I dinna
deny't,' I says, for the thing was well kent, ' but
ye'll do vara weel, Jeames,' says I, an' mairy him
I did."

" He was a harmless crittur, Jeames," said Haggart, " but queer. Ay, he was full o' maggots."

" Ay," said Jeames's widow, " but though it's
no' for me to say't, he deid a deacon."

" There's some rale queer wys o' speirin' a
wuman," began the mole-catcher.

" Vary true, Jamie," said a stone-breaker. " I
mind hoo — "

" There was a chappy ower by Blair," continued
Jamie, raising his voice, " 'at micht hae been a
single man to this day if it hadna been for the
toothache."

" Ay, man ? "

" Joey Fargus was the stock's name. He was oncommon troubled wi' the toothache till he found a cure."

" I didna ken o' ony cure for sair teeth ? "

" Joey's cure was to pour cauld watter stretcht on into his mooth for the maiter o' twa 'oors, an' ae day he cam into Blair an' found Jess McTaggart (a speerity bit thingy she was — ou, she was so) fair greetin' wi' sair teeth. Joey advised the crittur to try his cure, an' when he left she was pourin' the watter into her mooth ower the sink. Weel, it so happened 'at Joey was in Blair again aboot twa month after, an' he gies a cry in at Willie's — that's Jess's father's, as ye'll un'erstan'. Ay, then, Jess had haen anither fit o' the toothache, an' she was hingin' ower the sink wi' a tanker o' watter in her han', juist as she'd been when he saw her last. ' What!' says Joey, wi' rale consairn, ' nae better yet ?' The stock thocht she had been haddin' gaen at the watter a' thae twa month."

" I call to mind," the stone-breaker broke in again, " hoo a body — "

" So," continued Jamie, " Joey cudna help but admire the patience o' the lassie, an' says he, ' Jess,' he says, ' come oot by to Mortar Pits, an' try oor well.' That's hoo Joey Fargus speired's wife, an' if ye dinna believe's, ye've nae mair to do but ging to Mortar Pits an' see the well yersels."

"I recall," said the stone-breaker, "a very neat case o' speirin'. It was Jocky Wilkie, him 'at's brither was grieve to Broken Busses, an' the lass was Leeby Lunan. She was aye puttin' Jocky aff when he was on the point o' speirin' her, keepin' 'im hingin' on the hook like a trout, as ye may say, an' takkin' her fling wi' ither lads at the same time."

"Ay, I've kent them do that."

"Weel, it fair maddened Jocky, so ae nicht he gings to her father's hoose wi' a present o' a grand thimble to her in his pooch, an' afore the hale hoosehold he perdooces't an' flings't wi' a bang on the dresser: 'Tak it,' he says to Leeby, 'or leave't.' In coorse the thing's bein' done sae public-like, Leeby kent she had to mak up her mind there an' then. Ay, she took it."

"But hoo did ye speir Chirsty yersel, Dan'l?" asked Jinny of the speaker.

There was a laugh at this, for, as was well known, Dan'l had jilted Chirsty.

"I never kent I had speired," replied the stone-breaker, "till Chirsty told me."

"Ye'll no' say ye wasna fond o' her?"

"Sometimes I was, an' syne at other times I was indifferent-like. The mair I thocht o't the mair risky I saw it was, so 'i the tail o' the day I says to Chirsty, says I, 'Na, na, Chirsty, lat's be as I am.'"

"They say she took on terrible, Dan'l."

"Ay, nae doot, but a man has 'imself to con-seeder."

By this time they had crossed the moor of whins. It was a cold, still evening, and as they paused before climbing down into the town they heard the tinkle of a bell.

"That's Snecky's bell," said the mole-catcher; "what can he be cryin' at this time o' nicht?"

"There's something far wrang," said one of the women. "Look, a'body's rinnin' to the square."

The troubled look returned to Tammas Haggart's face, and he stopped to look back across the fast darkening moor.

"Did ony o' ye see little Davy Dundas, the saw-miller's bairny?" he began.

At that moment a young man swept by. His teeth were clenched, his eyes glaring.

"Speak o' the deil," said the mole-catcher; "that was Rob Angus."

CHAPTER II

ROB BECOMES FREE

As Haggart hobbled down into the square, in the mole-catcher's rear, Hobart's cracked bell tinkled up the back-wynd, and immediately afterwards the bellman took his stand by the side of Tam Peter's fish-cart. Snecky gave his audience time to gather, for not every day was it given him to cry a lost bairn. The words fell slowly from his reluctant lips. Before he flung back his head and ejected his proclamation in a series of puffs he was the possessor of exclusive news, but his tongue had hardly ceased to roll round the concluding sentence when the crowd took up the cry themselves. Wives flinging open their windows shouted their fears across the wynds. Davy Dundas had wandered from the kirkyard, where Rob had left her in Kitty Wilkie's charge till he returned from the woods. What had Kitty been about? It was believed that the litlin had taken with her a letter that had come for Rob. Was Rob back from the woods yet? Ay, he had scoured the whole countryside already for her.

ROB BECOMES FREE

Men gathered on the saw-mill brig, looking perplexedly at the burn that swirled at this point, a sawdust colour, between wooden boards; but the women pressed their bairns closely to their wrappers and gazed in each other's faces.

A log of wood, with which some one had sought to improvise a fire between the bricks that narrowed Rob Angus's grate, turned peevishly to charcoal without casting much light on the men and women in the saw-mill kitchen. Already the burn had been searched near the mill, with Rob's white face staring at the searchers from his door.

The room was small and close. A closet-bed with the door off afforded seats for several persons; and Davit Lunan, the tinsmith, who could read Homer with Rob in the original, sat clumsily on the dresser. The pendulum of a wag-at-the-wa' clock swung silently against the wall, casting a mouse-like shadow on the hearth. Over the mantelpiece was a sampler in many colours, the work of Rob's mother when she was still a maid. The book-case, fitted into a recess that had once held a press, was Rob's own handiwork, and contained more books than any other house in Thrums. Overhead the thick wooden rafters were crossed with saws and staves.

There was a painful silence in the gloomy room. Snecky Hobart tried to break the log in the fireplace, using his leg as a poker, but desisted when he saw every eye turned on him. A glitter of sparks shot up the chimney, and the starling in the window began to whistle. Pete Todd looked undecidedly at the minister, and, lifting a sack, flung it over the bird's cage, as if anticipating the worst. In Thrums they veil their cages if there is a death in the house.

"What do ye mean, Pete Todd?" cried Rob Angus, fiercely.

His voice broke, but he seized the sack and cast it on the floor. The starling, however, whistled no more.

Looking as if he could strike Pete Todd, Rob stood in the centre of his kitchen, a saw-miller for the last time. Though they did not know it, his neighbours there were photographing him in their minds, and their children were destined to gape in the days to come over descriptions of Rob Angus in corduroys.

These pictures showed a broad-shouldered man of twenty-six, whose face was already rugged. A short brown beard hid the heavy chin, and the lips were locked as if Rob feared to show that he was anxious about the child. His clear gray eyes were younger-looking than his forehead, and the swollen balls beneath them suggested a student rather than a working man. His hands were too tanned and hard ever to be white, and he delved a little in his walk, as if he felt uncomfortable without a weight on his back. He was the best saw-miller in his county, but his ambition would have scared his customers had he not kept it to himself. Many a time strangers had stared at him as he strode along the Whunny road, and wondered what made this stalwart man whirl the axe that he had been using as a staff. Then Rob was thinking of the man he was going to be when he could safely leave little Davy behind him, and it was not the firs of the Whunny wood that were in his eye, but a roaring city and a saw-miller taking it by the throat. There had been a time when he bore no love for the bairn who came between him and his career.

Rob was so tall that he could stand erect in but few rooms in Thrums, and long afterwards, when very different doors opened to him, he still involuntarily ducked, as he crossed a threshold, to save his head. Up to the day on which Davy wandered from home he had never lifted his hat to a lady; when he did that the influence of Thrums would be broken for ever.

" It's oncommon foolish o' Rob," said Pete Todd, retreating to the side of the mole-catcher, " no' to be mair resigned-like."

" It's his ind'pendence," answered Jamie; " ay, the wricht was sayin' the noo, says he, ' If Davy's deid, Rob'll mak the coffin 'imsel, he's sae michty ind'pendent.' "

Tammas Haggart stumbled into the saw-miller's

kitchen. It would have been a womanish kind of thing to fling to the door behind him.

"Fine growin' day, Rob," he said, deliberately.

"It is so, Tammas," answered the saw-miller, hospitably, for Haggart had been his father's bosom friend.

"No' much drowth, I'm thinkin'," said Hobart, relieved by the turn the conversation had taken.

Tammas pulled from beneath the table an unsteady three-legged stool — Davy's stool — and sat down on it slowly. Rob took a step nearer as if to ask him to sit somewhere else, and then turned away his head.

"Ay, ay," said Haggart.

Then, as he saw the others gathering round the minister at the door, he moved uneasily on his stool.

"Whaur's Davy?" he said.

"Did ye no' ken she was lost?" the saw-miller asked, in a voice that was hardly his own.

"Ay, I kent," said Tammas; "she's on the Whunny road."

Rob had been talking to the minister in what both thought English, which in Thrums is considered an ostentatious language, but he turned on Tammas in broad Scotch. In the years to come, when he could wear gloves without concealing his hands in his pockets, excitement brought on Scotch as a poultice raises blisters.

"Tammas Haggart," he cried, pulling the stone-breaker off his stool.

The minister interposed.

"Tell us what you know at once, Tammas," said Mr. Dishart, who, out of the pulpit, had still a heart.

It was a sad tale that Haggart had to tell, if a short one, and several of the listeners shook their heads as they heard it.

"I meant to turn the lassieky," the stone-breaker explained, "but, ou, she was past in a twinklin'."

On the saw-mill brig the minister quickly organized a search party, the brig that Rob had floored anew but the week before, rising daily with the sun to do it because the child's little boot had caught in a worn board. From it she had often crooned to watch the dank mill-wheel climbing the bouncing burn. Ah, Rob, the rotten old planks would have served your turn.

"The Whunny road," were the words passed from mouth to mouth, and the driblet of men fell into line.

Impetuous is youth, and the minister was not perhaps greatly to blame for starting at once. But Lang Tammas, his chief elder, paused on the threshold.

"The Lord giveth," he said, solemnly, taking off his hat and letting the night air cut through his white hair, "and the Lord taketh away: blessed be the name of the Lord."

25

WHEN A MAN'S SINGLE

The saw-miller opened his mouth, but no words came.

The little search party took the cold Whunny road. The day had been bright and fine, and still there was a smell of flowers in the air. The fickle flowers! They had clustered round Davy and nestled on her neck when she drew the half-ashamed saw-miller through the bleating meadows, and now they could smile on him when he came alone — all except the daisies. The daisies, that cannot play a child false, had craned their necks to call Davy back as she tripped over them, and bowed their heavy little heads as she toddled on. It was from them that the bairn's track was learned after she wandered from the Whunny road.

By and by the hills ceased to echo their wailing response to Hobart's bell.

Far in the rear of the more eager searchers, the bellman and the joiner had found a seat on a mossy bank, and others, footsore and weary, had fallen elsewhere from the ranks. The minister and half a dozen others scattered over the fields and on the hillsides, despondent, but not daring to lag. Tinkers cowered round their kettles under threatening banks, and the squirrels were shadows gliding from tree to tree.

At a distant smithy a fitful light still winked to the wind, but the farm lamps were out and all the

26

land was hushed. It was now long past midnight in country parts.

Rob Angus was young and strong, but the heaven-sent gift of tears was not for him. Blessed the moaning mother by the cradle of her eldest-born, and the maid in tears for the lover who went out so brave in the morning and was not at even-fall, and the weeping sister who can pray for her soldier brother, and the wife on her husband's bosom.

Some of his neighbours had thought it unmanly when Rob, at the rumble of a cart, hurried from the saw-mill to snatch the child in his arms, and bear her to a bed of shavings. At such a time Davy would lift a saw to within an inch of her baby-face, and then, letting it fall with a wicked chuckle, run to the saw-miller's arms, as sure of her lover as ever maiden was of man.

A bashful lover he had been, shy, not of Davy, but of what men would say, and now the time had come when he looked wistfully back to a fevered child tossing in a dark bed, the time when a light burned all night in Rob's kitchen, and a trembling heavy-eyed man sat motionless on a high-backed chair. How noiselessly he approached the bonny mite and replaced the arm that had wandered from beneath the coverlet! Ah, for the old time when a sick imperious child told her uncle to lie down beside her, and Rob sat on the bed, looking shamefacedly at the minister. Mr. Dishart had turned away his head. Such things are not to be told. They are between a man and his God.

Far up the Whunny hill they found Davy's little shoe. Rob took it in his hand, a muddy, draggled shoe that had been a pretty thing when he put it on her foot that morning. The others gathered austerely around him, and strong Rob stood still among the brackens.

"I'm dootin' she's deid," said Tammas Haggart.

Haggart looked in the face of old Rob's son, and then a strange and beautiful thing happened. To the wizened stone-breaker it was no longer the sombre Whunny hill that lay before him. Two barefooted herd-laddies were on the green fields of adjoining farms. The moon looking over the hills found them on their ragged backs, with the cows munching by their side. They had grown different boys, nor known why, among the wild roses of red and white, and trampling neck-high among the ferns. Haggart saw once again the raspberry bushes they had stripped together into flagons gleaming in the grass. Rob had provided the bent pin with which Tammas lured his first trout to land, and Tammas in return had invited him to thraw the neck of a doomed hen. They had wandered hand-in-hand through thirsty grass, when scythes whistled in the corn-fields, and larks trilled overhead, and braes were golden with broom.

28

ROB BECOMES FREE

They are two broad-shouldered men now, and Haggart's back is rounding at the loom. From his broken window he can see Rob at the saw-mill, whistling as the wheel goes around. It is Saturday night, and they are in the square, clean and dapper, talking with other gallants about lasses. They are courting the same maid, and she sits on a stool by the door, knitting a stocking, with a lover on each side. They drop in on her mother straining the blaeberry juice through a bag suspended between two chairs. They sheepishly admire while Easie singes a hen; for love of her they help her father to pit his potatoes; and then, for love of the other, each gives her up. It is a Friday night, and from a but and ben around which the rabble heave and toss, a dozen couples emerge in strangely gay and bright apparel. Rob leads the way with one lass, and Tammas follows with another. It must be Rob's wedding-day.

Dim grow Tammas's eyes on the Whunny hill. The years whirl by, and already he sees a grumpy gravedigger go out to dig Rob's grave. Alas! for the flash into the past that sorrow gives. As he clutches young Rob's hand the light dies from Tammas's eyes, his back grows round and bent, and the hair is silvered that lay in tousled locks on a lad's head.

A nipping wind cut the search party and fled down the hill that was changing in colour from black to grey. The searchers might have been smugglers laden with whisky bladders, such as haunted the mountain in bygone days. Far away at Thrums mothers still wrung their hands for Davy, but the men slept.

Heads were bared, and the minister raised his voice in prayer. One of the psalms of David trembled in the grey of the morning straight to heaven; and then two young men, glancing at Mr. Dishart, raised aloft a fallen rowan-tree, to let it fall as it listed. It fell pointing straight down the hill, and the search party took that direction; all but Rob, who stood motionless, with the shoe in his hand. He did not seem to comprehend the minister's beckoning.

Haggart took him by the arm.

" Rob, man, Rob Angus," he said, " she was but fower year auld."

The stone-breaker unbuttoned his trouser-pocket, and with an unsteady hand drew out his snuff-mull. Rob tried to take it, but his arm trembled, and the mull fell among the heather.

"Keep yourselves from idols," said Lang Tammas, sternly.

But the minister was young, and children lisped his name at the white manse among the trees at home. He took the shoe from the saw-miller who had once been independent. and they went down the hill together.

Davy lay dead at the edge of the burn that gurgles on to the saw-mill, one little foot washed by the stream. The Whunny had rocked her to sleep for the last time. Half covered with grass, her baby-fist still clutched the letter. When Rob saw her, he took his darling dead bairn in his arms and faced the others with cracking jaws.

"I dinna ken," said Tammas Haggart, after a pause, "but what it's kind of nat'ral."

CHAPTER III

ONE evening, nearly a month after Rob Angus became "single," Mr. George Frederick Licquorish, editor and proprietor of the *Silchester Mirror*, was sitting in his office cutting advertisements out of the *Silchester Argus*, and pasting each on a separate sheet of paper. These advertisements had not been sent to the *Mirror*, and, as he thought this a pity, he meant, through his canvasser, to call the attention of the advertisers to the omission.

Mr. Licquorish was a stout little man, with a benevolent countenance, who wrote most of his leaders on the backs of old envelopes. Every few minutes he darted into the composing-room, with an alertness that was a libel on his genial face; and when he returned it was pleasant to observe the kindly, good-natured manner in which he chaffed the printer's devil who was trying to light the fire. It was, however, also noticeable that what the devil said subsequently to another devil was — "But, you know, he wouldn't give me any sticks."

ROB GOES OUT INTO THE WORLD

The *Mirror* and the *Argus* are two daily news-papers published in Silchester, each of which has the largest circulation in the district, and is therefore much the better advertising medium. Silchester is the chief town of an English midland county, and the *Mirror's* business note-paper refers to it as the centre of a population of half a million souls.

The *Mirror's* offices are nearly crushed out of sight in a block of buildings, left in the middle of a street for town councils to pull down gradually. This island of houses, against which a sea of humanity beats daily, is cut in two by a narrow passage, off which several doors open. One of these leads up a dirty stair to the editorial and composing-rooms of the *Daily Mirror*, and down a dirty stair to its printing-rooms. It is the door at which you may hammer for an hour without any one's paying the least attention.

During the time the boy took to light Mr. Licquorish's fire, a young man in a heavy over-coat knocked more than once at the door in the alley, and then moved off as if somewhat relieved that there was no response. He walked round and round the block of buildings, gazing upwards at the windows of the composing-room; and several times he ran against other pedestrians on whom he turned fiercely, and would then have begged their pardons had he known what to say. Frequently he felt in his pocket to see if his money was still there, and once he went behind a door and counted it. There was three pounds seventeen shillings altogether, and he kept it in a linen bag that had been originally made for carrying worms in when he went fishing. When he re-entered the close he always drew a deep breath, and if any persons emerged from the *Mirror* office he looked after them. They were mostly telegraph boys, who fluttered out and in.

When Mr. Licquorish dictated an article, as he did frequently, the apprentice-reporter went into the editor's room to take it down, and the reporters always asked him, as a favour, to shut George Frederick's door behind him. This apprentice-reporter did the police reports and the magazine notices, and he wondered a good deal whether the older reporters really did like brandy and soda. The reason why John Milton, which was the unfortunate name of this boy, was told to close the editorial door behind him was that it was close to the door of the reporters' room, and generally stood open. The impression the reporters' room made on a chance visitor varied according as Mr. Licquorish's door was ajar or shut. When they heard it locked on the inside, the reporters and the subeditor breathed a sigh of relief; when it opened they took their legs off the desk.

The editor's room had a carpet, and was chiefly

furnished with books sent in for review. It was more comfortable, but more gloomy-looking than the reporters' room, which had a long desk running along one side of it, and a bunk for holding coals and old newspapers on the other side. The floor was so littered with papers, many of them still in their wrappers, that, on his way between his seat and the door, the reporter generally kicked one or more into the bunk. It was in this way, unless an apprentice happened to be otherwise disengaged, that the floor was swept.

In this room were a reference library and an old coat. The library was within reach of the sub-editor's hand, and contained some fifty books, which the literary staff could consult, with the conviction that they would find the page they wanted missing. The coat had hung unbrushed on a nail for many years, and was so thick with dust that John Milton could draw pictures on it with his finger. According to legend, it was the coat of a distinguished novelist, who had once been a reporter on the *Mirror*, and had left Silchester unostentatiously by his window.

It was Penny, the foreman in the composing-room, who set the literary staff talking about the new reporter. Penny was a lank, loosely jointed man of forty, who shuffled about the office in slippers, ruled the compositors with a loud voice and a blustering manner, and was believed to be in Mr. Licquorish's confidence. His politics were respect for the House of Lords, because it rose early, enabling him to have it set before supper-time.

The foreman slithered so quickly from one room to another that he was at the sub-editor's elbow before his own door had time to shut. There was some copy in his hand, and he flung it contempt-uously upon the desk.

" Look here, Mister," he said, flinging the copy upon the sub-editor's desk, " I don't want that."

The sub-editor was twisted into as little space as possible, tearing telegrams open and flinging the envelopes aside, much as a housewife shells peas. His name was Protheroe, and the busier he was the more he twisted himself. On Budget nights he was a knot. He did voluntarily so much extra work that Mr. Licquorish often thought he gave him too high wages; and on slack nights he smiled to himself, which showed that something pleased him. It was rather curious that this something should have been himself.

" But — but," cried Protheroe, all in a flutter, " it's town council meeting; it — it must be set, Mr. Penny."

" Very well, Mister; then that special from Bir-mingham must be slaughtered."

" No, no, Mr. Penny; why, that's a speech by Bright."

Penny sneered at the sub-editor, and flung up his arms to imply that he washed his hands of the whole thing, as he had done every night for the last ten years, when there was pressure on his space. Protheroe had been there for half of that time, yet he still trembled before the autocrat of the office.

"There's enough copy on the board," said Penny, " to fill the paper. Any more specials coming in ? "

He asked this fiercely, as if of opinion that the sub-editor arranged with leading statesmen nightly to flood the composing-room of the *Mirror* with speeches. and Protheroe replied abjectly, as if he had been caught doing it — " Lord John Manners is speaking to-night at Nottingham."

The foreman dashed his hand upon the desk.

"Go it, Mister, go it," he cried; "anything else ? Tell me Gladstone's dead next."

Sometimes about two o'clock in the morning Penny would get sociable, and the sub-editor was always glad to respond. On those occasions they talked with bated breath of the amount of copy that would come in should anything happen to Mr. Gladstone; and the sub-editor, if he was in a despondent mood, predicted that it would occur at midnight. Thinking of this had made him a Conservative.

" Nothing so bad as that," he said, dwelling on

the subject, to show the foreman that they might
be worse off; "but there's a column of local coming in, and a concert in the People's Hall, and —"

"And you expect me to set all that ?" the foreman broke in. " Why, the half of that local should
have been set by seven o'clock, and here I've only
got the beginning of the town council yet. It's
ridiculous."

Protheroe looked timidly towards the only reporter present, and then apologetically towards
Penny for having looked at the reporter.

"The stuff must be behind," growled Tomlinson, nicknamed Umbrage, "as long as we're a man
short."

Umbrage was very short and stout, with a big
moon face, and always wore his coat unbuttoned.
In the streets, if he was walking fast and there was
a breeze, his coat-tails seemed to be running after
him. He squinted a little, from a habit he had of
looking sideways at public meetings to see if the
audience was gazing at him. He was " Juvenal "
in the *Mirror* on Friday mornings, and headed his
column of local gossip which had that signature,
" Now step I forth to whip hypocrisy."

" I wonder," said the sub-editor, with an insinuat-
ing glance at the foreman, "if the new man is expected to-night."

Mr. Licquorish had told him that this was so an
hour before, but the cunning bred of fear advised

him to give Penny the opportunity of divulging the news.

That worthy smiled to himself, as any man has a right to do who has been told something in confidence by his employer.

" He's a Yorkshireman, I believe," continued the crafty Protheroe.

" That's all you know," said the foreman, first glancing back to see if Mr. Licquorish's door was shut. " Mr. George Frederick has told me all about him; he's a Scotsman called Angus that's never been out of his native county."

" He's one of those compositors taken to literature, is he ? " asked Umbrage, who by literature meant reporting, pausing in the middle of a sentence he was transcribing from his note-book. " Just as I expected," he added, contemptuously.

" No," said the foreman, thawing in the rays of such ignorance; " Mr. George Frederick says he's never been on a newspaper before."

" An outsider ! " cried Umbrage, in the voice with which outsiders themselves would speak of reptiles. " They are the ruin of the profession, they are."

" He'll make you all sit up, Mister," said Penny, with a chuckle. " Mr. George Frederick has had his eye on him for a twelvemonth."

" I don't suppose you know how Mr. George Frederick fell in with him ? " said the sub-editor, basking in Penny's geniality.

"Mr. George Frederick told me everythink about him — everythink," said the foreman, proudly. "It was a parson that recommended him."

"A parson!" ejaculated Umbrage, in such a tone that if you had not caught the word you might have thought he was saying "An outsider!" again.

"Yes, a parson whose sermon this Angus took down in shorthand, I fancy."

"What was he doing taking down a sermon?"

"I suppose he was there to hear it."

"And this is the kind of man who is taking to literature nowadays!" Umbrage cried.

"O, Mr. George Frederick has heard a great deal about aim," continued Penny, maliciously, "and expects him to do wonders. He's a self-made man."

"O," said Umbrage, who could find nothing to object to in that, having risen from comparative obscurity himself.

"Mr. George Frederick," Penny went on, "offered him a berth here before Billy Tagg was engaged, but he couldn't come."

"I suppose," said Juvenal, with the sarcasm that made him terrible on Fridays, "the *Times* offered him something better, or was it the *Spectator* that wanted an editor?"

"No, it was family matters. His mother or his

sister, or— let me see, it was his sister's child —
was dependent on him, and could not be left.
Something happened to her, though. She's dead,
I think, so he's a free man now."

" Yes, it was his sister's child, and she was found
dead," said the sub-editor, " on a mountain-side,
curiously enough, with George Frederick's letter
in her hand offering Angus the appointment."

Protheroe was foolish to admit that he knew this,
for it was news to the foreman, but it tries a man
severely to have to listen to news that he could tell
better himself. One immediate result of the sub-
editor's rashness was that Rob Angus sunk several
stages in Penny's estimation.

" I daresay he'll turn out a muff," he said, and
flung out of the room, with another intimation that
the copy must be cut down.

The evening wore on. Protheroe had half a
dozen things to do at once, and did them.

Telegraph boys were dropping the beginning of
lord John Manners's speech through a grating on
to the sub-editorial desk long before he had reached
the end of it at Nottingham.

The sub-editor had to revise this as it arrived in
flimsy, and write a summary of it at the same time.
His summary was set before all the speech had
reached the office, which may seem strange. But
when Penny cried aloud for summary, so that he
might get that column off his hands, Protheroe

made guesses at many things, and, risking, "the right hon. gentleman concluded his speech, which was attentively listened to, with some further references to current topics," flung Lord John to the boy, who rushed with him to Penny, from whose hand he was snatched by a compositor. Fifteen minutes afterwards Lord John concluded his speech at Nottingham.

About half-past nine Protheroe seized his hat and rushed home for supper. In the passage he nearly knocked himself over by running against the young man in the heavy top-coat. Umbrage went out to see if he could gather any information about a prize-fight. John Milton came in with a notice of a concert, which he stuck conspicuously on the chief reporter's file. When the chief reporter came in, he glanced through it and made a few alterations, changing " Mr. Joseph Grimes sang out of tune," for instance, to " Mr. Grimes, the favourite vocalist, was in excellent voice." The concert was not quite over yet, either ; they seldom waited for the end of anything on the *Mirror*.

When Umbrage returned, Billy Kirker, the chief reporter, was denouncing John Milton for not being able to tell him how to spell "deceive."

" What is the use of you ? " he asked, indignantly, " if you can't do a simple thing like that ? "

" Say ' cheat '," suggested Umbrage.

So Kirker wrote " cheat." Though he was the

42

chief of the *Mirror's* reporting department, he had only Umbrage and John Milton at present under him.

As Kirker sat in the reporters' room looking over his diary, with a cigarette in his mouth, he was an advertisement for the *Mirror*, and if he paid for his velvet coat out of his salary, the paper was in a healthy financial condition. He was tall, twenty-two years of age, and extremely slight. His manner was languid, though his language was sometimes forcible, but those who knew him did not think him mild. This evening his fingers looked bare without the diamond ring that sometimes adorned them. This ring, it was noticed, generally disappeared about the middle of the month, and his scarf-pin followed it by the twenty-first. With the beginning of the month they reappeared together. The literary staff was paid monthly.

Mr. Licquorish looked in at the door of the reporters' room to ask pleasantly if they would not like a fire. Had Protheroe been there he would have said "No"; but Billy Kirker said "Yes." Mr. Licquorish had thought that Protheroe was there.

This was the first fire in the reporters' room that season, and it smoked. Kirker, left alone, flung up the window, and gradually became aware that some one with a heavy tread was walking up and

43

down the alley. He whistled gently in case it should be a friend of his own, but, getting no response, resumed his work. Mr. Licquorish also heard the footsteps, but though he was waiting for the new reporter, he did not connect him with the man outside.

Rob had stopped at the door a score of times, and then turned away. He had arrived at Silchester in the afternoon, and come straight to the *Mirror* office to look at it. Then he had set out in quest of lodgings, and, having got them, had returned to the passage. He was not naturally a man crushed by a sense of his own unworthiness, but, looking up at these windows and at the shadows that passed them every moment, he felt far away from his saw-mill. What a romance to him, too, was in the glare of the gas and in the *Mirror* bill that was being reduced to pulp on the wall at the mouth of the close! It had begun to rain heavily, but he did not feel the want of an umbrella, never having possessed one in Thrums.

Fighting down the emotions that had mastered him so often, he turned once more to the door, and as he knocked more loudly than formerly, a compositor came out, who told him what to do if he was there on business.

"Go upstairs," he said, "till you come to a door, and then kick."

Rob did not have to kick, however, for he met

44

Mr. Licquorish coming downstairs, and both half stopped.

" Not Mr. Angus, is it ? " asked Mr. Licquorish.

" Yes," said the new reporter, the monosyllable also telling that he was a Scotsman, and that he did not feel comfortable.

Mr. Licquorish shook him warmly by the hand, and took him into the editor's room. Rob sat in a chair there with his hat in his hand, while his new employer spoke kindly to him about the work that would begin on the morrow.

" You will find it a little strange at first," he said; " but Mr. Kirker, the head of our reporting staff, has been instructed to explain the routine of the office to you, and I have no doubt we shall work well together."

Rob said he meant to do his best.

" It is our desire, Mr. Angus," continued Mr. Licquorish, " to place every facility before our staff, and if you have suggestions to make at any time on any matter connected with your work we shall be most happy to consider them and to meet you in a cordial spirit."

While Rob was thanking Mr. Licquorish for his consideration, Kirker in the next room was wondering whether the new reporter was to have half a crown a week less than his predecessor, who had begun with six pounds a month.

" It is pleasant to us," Mr. Licquorish concluded,

referring to the novelist, "to know that we have
sent out from this office a number of men who
subsequently took a high place in literature. Perhaps our system of encouraging talent by fostering
it has had something to do with this, for we like to
give every one his opportunity to rise. I hope the
day will come, Mr. Angus, when we shall be able
to recall with pride the fact that you began your
literary career on the *Mirror*."

Rob said he hoped so too. He had, indeed,
very little doubt of it. At this period of his career
it made him turn white to think that he might not
yet be famous.

"But I must not keep you here any longer,"
said the editor, rising, "for you have had a weary
journey, and must be feeling tired. We shall see
you at ten o'clock to-morrow?"

Once more Rob and his employer shook hands
heartily.

"But I might introduce you," said Mr. Licquorish, "to the reporting-room. Mr. Kirker, our chief,
is, I think, here."

Rob had begun to descend the stairs, but he
turned back. He was not certain what you did
when you were introduced to any one, such for-
malities being unknown in Thrums; but he held
himself in reserve to do as the other did.

"Ah, Mr. Kirker," said the editor, pushing open
the door of the reporting-room with his foot, "this

is Mr. Angus, who has just joined our literary staff."

Nodding genially to both, Mr. Licquorish darted out of the room ; but before the door had finished its swing, Mr. Kirker was aware that the new reporter's nails had a rim of black.

" What do you think of George Frederick ? " asked the chief, after he had pointed out to Rob the only chair that such a stalwart reporter might safely sit on.

" He was very pleasant," said Rob.

" Yes," said Billy Kirker, thoughtfully, " there's nothing George Frederick wouldn't do for any one if it could be done gratis."

" And he struck me as an enterprising sort of man."

" ' Enterprise without outlay,' is the motto of this office," said the chief.

" But the paper seems to be well conducted," said Rob, a little crestfallen.

" The worst conducted in England," said Kirker, cheerfully.

Rob asked how the *Mirror* compared with the *Argus*.

" They have six reporters to our three," said Kirker, " but we do double work and beat them."

" I suppose there is a great deal of rivalry between the staffs of the two papers ? " Rob asked, for he had read of such things.

"Oh no," said Kirker, "we help each other. For instance, if Daddy Walsh, the *Argus* chief, is drunk, I help him; and if I'm drunk, he helps me. I'm going down to the Frying Pan to see him now."

"The Frying Pan?" echoed Rob.

"It's a literary club," Kirker explained, "and very exclusive. If you come with me I'll introduce you."

Rob was somewhat taken aback at what he had heard, but he wanted to be on good terms with his fellow-workers.

"Not to-night," he said. "I think I'd better be getting home now."

Kirker lit another cigarette, and saying he would expect Rob at the office next morning, strolled off. The new reporter was undecided whether to follow him at once, or to wait for Mr. Licquorish's reappearance. He was looking round the office curiously, when the door opened and Kirker put his head in.

"By the by, old chap," he said, "could you lend me five bob?"

"Yes, yes," said the new reporter.

He had to undo the string of his money-bag, but the chief was too fine a gentleman to smile.

"Thanks, old man," Kirker said, carelessly, and again withdrew.

The door of the editor's room was open as Rob passed.

48

ROB GOES OUT INTO THE WORLD

" Ah, Mr. Angus," said Mr. Licquorish, " here are a number of books for review; you might do a short notice of some of them."

He handed Rob the two works that happened to lie uppermost, and the new reporter slipped them into his pockets with a certain elation. The night was dark and wet, but he lit his pipe and hurried up the muddy streets to the single room that was now his home. Probably his were the only lodgings in his street that had not the portrait of a young lady on the mantelpiece. On his way he passed three noisy young men. They were Kirker and two reporters on the *Argus* trying which could fling his hat highest in the rain.

Sitting in his lonely room Rob examined his books with interest. One of them was Tennyson's new volume of poems, and a month afterwards the poet laureate's publishers made Rob march up the streets of Silchester with his chest well forward by advertising " The *Silchester Mirror* says, ' This admirable volume.' " After all, the great delight of being on the press is that you can patronize the Tennysons. Doubtless the poet laureate got a marked copy of Rob's first review forwarded him, and had an anxious moment till he saw that it was favourable. There had been a time when even John Milton felt a thrill pass through him as he saw Messrs. Besant and Rice boasting that he thought their " Chaplain of the Fleet " a novel of sustained interest, "which we have read without fatigue."

Rob sat over his empty grate far on into the night, his mind in a jumble. As he grew more composed the *Mirror* and its staff sank out of sight, and he was carrying a dead child in his arms along the leafy Whunny road. His mouth twitched, and his head drooped. He was preparing to go to bed when he sat down again to look at the other book. It was a novel by "M." in one thin volume, and Rob thought the title, "The Scorn of Scorns," foolish. He meant to write an honest criticism of it, but never having reviewed a book before, he rather hoped that this would be a poor one, which he could condemn brilliantly. Poor Rob! he came to think more of that book by and by.

At last Rob wound up the big watch that neighbours had come to gaze at when his father bought it of a pedlar forty years before, and took off the old silver chain that he wore round his neck. He went down on his knees to say his prayers, and then, remembering that he had said them already, rose up and went to bed.

CHAPTER IV

St. Leonard's Lodge is the residence of Mr. William Meredith, an ex-mayor of Silchester, and stands in the fashionable suburb of the town. There was at one time considerable intercourse between this house and Dome Castle, the seat of Colonel Abinger, though they are five miles apart and in different counties; and one day, after Rob had been on the press for a few months, two boys set out from the castle to show themselves to Nell Meredith. They could have reached the high-road by a private walk between a beach and an ivy hedge, but they preferred to climb down a steep path to the wild running Dome. The advantage of this route was that they risked their necks by taking it.

Nell, who did not expect visitors, was sitting by the fire in her boudoir dreaming. It was the room in which she and Mary Abinger had often discussed such great questions as Woman, her Aims, her Influence; Man, his Instability, his Weakness, his Degeneration; the Poor, how are

51

we to Help them; why Lady Lucy Gilding wears Pink when Blue is obviously her Colour.

Nell was tucked away into a soft armchair, in which her father never saw her without wondering that such a little thing should require eighteen yards for a dress.

" I'm not so little," she would say on these occasions, and then Mr. Meredith chuckled, for he knew that there were young men who considered his Nell tall and terrible. He liked to watch her sweeping through a room. To him the boudoir was a sea of reefs. Nell's dignity when she was introduced to a young gentleman was another thing her father could never look upon without awe, but he also noticed that it soon wore off.

On the mantelpiece lay a comb and several hair-pins. There are few more mysterious things than hair-pins. So far back as we can go into the past we see woman putting up her hair. It is said that married men lose their awe of hair-pins and clean their pipes with them.

A pair of curling-tongs had a chair to themselves near Nell, and she wore a short blue dressing-jacket. Probably when she woke from her reverie she meant to do something to her brown hair. When old gentlemen called at the lodge they frequently told their host that he had a very pretty daughter; when younger gentlemen called they generally called again, and if Nell thought they admired her the first time, she spared no pains to make them admire her still more the next time. This was to make them respect their own judgment.

It was little Will Abinger who had set Nell a-dreaming, for from wondering if he was home yet for the Christmas holidays her thoughts wandered to his sister Mary, and then to his brother Dick. She thought longer of Dick in his lonely London chambers than of the others, and by and by she was saying to herself petulantly, " I wish people wouldn't go dying and leaving me money." Mr. Meredith, and still more Mrs. Meredith, thought that their only daughter, an heiress, would be thrown away on Richard Abinger, barrister-at-law, whose blood was much bluer than theirs, but who was, nevertheless, understood to be as hard up as his father.

The door-bell rang, and two callers were ushered into the drawing-room without Nell's knowing it. One of them left his companion to talk to Mrs. Meredith, and clattered upstairs in search of the daughter of the house. He was a bright-faced boy of thirteen, with a passion for flinging stones, and, of late, he had worn his head in the air, not because he was conceited, but that he might look with admiration upon the face of the young gentleman downstairs.

Bouncing into the parlour, he caught sight of the object of his search before she could turn her head.

"I say, Nell, I'm back."

Miss Meredith jumped from her chair.

"Will!" she cried.

When the visitor saw this young lady coming toward him quickly, he knew what she was after, and tried to get out of her way. But Nell kissed him.

"Now, then," he said, indignantly, pushing her from him.

Will looked round him fearfully, and then closed the door.

"You might have waited till the door was shut, at any rate," he grumbled. "It would have been a nice thing if any one had seen you!"

"Why, what would it have mattered, you horrid little boy!" said Nell.

"Little boy! I'm bigger than you, at any rate. As for its not mattering — but you don't know who is downstairs. The captain — "

"Captain!" cried Nell.

She seized her curling-tongs.

"Yes," said Will, watching the effect of his words, "Greybrooke, the captain of the school. He is giving me a week just now."

Will said this as proudly as if his guest was Napoleon Bonaparte, but Nell laid down her curling-irons. The intruder interpreted her action and resented it.

"You're not his style," he said; "he likes bigger women."

"Oh, does he?" said Nell, screwing up her little Greek nose contemptuously.

"He's eighteen," said Will.

"A mere schoolboy."

"Why, he shaves."

"Doesn't the master whip him for that?"

"What? Whip Greybrooke!"

Will laughed hysterically.

"You should just see him at breakfast with old Jerry. Why, I've seen him myself, when half a dozen of us were asked to tea by Mrs. Jerry, and though we were frightened to open our mouths, what do you think Greybrooke did?"

"Something silly, I should say."

"He asked old Jerry, as cool as you like, to pass the butter! That's the sort of fellow Greybrooke is."

"How is Mary?"

"Oh, she's all right. No, she has a headache. I say, Greybrooke says Mary's rather slow."

"He must be a horror," said Nell, "and I don't see why you brought him here."

"I thought you would like to see him," explained Will. "He made a hundred and three against Rugby, and was only bowled off his pads."

"Well," said Nell, yawning, "I suppose I must go down and meet your prodigy."

Will, misunderstanding, got between her and the door.

"You're not going down like that," he said, anxiously, with a wave of his hand that included the dressing-jacket and the untidy hair. " Greybrooke's so particular, and I told him you were a jolly girl."

" What else did you tell him? " asked Nell, suspiciously.

"Not much," said Will, with a guilty look.

" I know you told him something else? "

" I told him you — you were fond of kissing people."

" Oh, you nasty boy, Will—as if kissing a child like you counted! "

"Never mind," said Will, soothingly, " Greybrooke's not the fellow to tell tales. Besides, I know you girls can't help it. Mary's just the same."

" You are a goose, Will, and the day will come when you'll give anything for a kiss."

" You've no right to bring such charges against a fellow," said Will, indignantly, strutting to the door.

Half-way downstairs he turned and came back.

" I say, Nell," he said, " You — you, when you come down, you won't kiss Greybrooke? "

Nell drew herself up in a way that would have scared any young man but Will.

" He's so awfully particular," Will continued, apologetically.

" Was it to tell me this you came upstairs? "

"No, honour bright, it wasn't. I only came up in case you should want to kiss me, and to — to have it over."

Nell was standing near Will, and before he could jump back she slapped his face.

The snow was dancing outside in a light wind when Nell sailed into the drawing-room. She could probably still inform you how she was dressed, but that evening Will and the captain could not tell Mary. The captain thought it was a reddish dress or else blue; but it was all in squares like a draught-board, according to Will. Forty minutes had elapsed since Will visited her upstairs, and now he smiled at the conceit which made her think that the captain would succumb to a pretty frock. Of course Nell had no such thought. She always dressed carefully because — well, because there is never any saying.

Though Miss Meredith froze Greybrooke with a glance, he was relieved to see her. Her mother had discovered that she knew the lady who married his brother, and had asked questions about the baby. He did not like it. These, he thought, were things you should pretend not to know about. He had contrived to keep his nieces and nephews dark from the fellows at school, though most of them would have been too just to attach any blame to him. Of this baby he was specially ashamed, because they had called it after him.

WHEN A MAN'S SINGLE

Mrs. Meredith was a small, stout lady, of whose cleverness her husband spoke proudly to Nell, but never to herself. When Nell told her how he had talked, she exclaimed, "Nonsense!" and then waited to hear what else he had said. She loved him, but probably no woman can live with a man for many years without having an indulgent contempt for him, and wondering how he is considered a good man of business. Mrs. Meredith, who was a terribly active woman, was glad to leave the entertainment of her visitors to Nell, and that young lady began severely by asking "how you boys mean to amuse yourselves?"

"Do you keep rabbits?" she said to the captain, sweetly.

"I say, Nell!" cried Will, warningly.

"I have not kept rabbits," Greybrooke replied, with simple dignity, "since I was a boy."

"I told you," said Will, "that Greybrooke was old — why, he's nearly as old as yourself. She's older than she looks, you know, Greybrooke."

The captain was gazing at Nell with intense admiration. As she raised her head indignantly he thought she was looking to him for protection. That was a way Nell had.

"Abinger," said the captain, sternly, "shut up."

"Don't mind him, Miss Meredith," he continued; "he doesn't understand girls."

To think he understands girls is the last affront

a youth pays them. When he ceases trying to reduce them to fixed principles he has come of age. Nell, knowing this, felt sorry for Greybrooke, for she foresaw what he would have to go through. Her manner to him underwent such a change that he began to have a high opinion of himself. This is often called falling in love. Will was satisfied that his friend impressed Nell, and he admired Greybrooke's politeness to a chit of a girl, but he became restless. His eyes wandered to the piano, and he had a lurking fear that Nell would play something. He signed to the captain to get up.

" We'll have to be going now," he said at last; " good-bye."

Greybrooke glared at Will, forgetting that they had arranged beforehand to stay as short a time as possible.

" Perhaps you have other calls to make ? " said Nell, who had no desire to keep them there longer than they cared to stay.

" Oh, yes," said Will.

" No," said the captain, " we only came into Silchester with Miss Abinger's message for you."

" Why, Will," exclaimed Nell, " you never gave me any message ? "

" I forgot what it was," Will explained, cheerily; " something about a ribbon, I think."

" I did not hear the message given," the captain said, in answer to Nell's look, " but Miss Abinger had a headache, and I think Will said it had to do with that."

"Oh, wait a bit," said Will, "I remember something about it now. Mary saw something in a Silchester paper, the *Mirror*, I think, that made her cry, and she thinks that if you saw it you would cry too. So she wants you to look at it."

"The idea of Mary's crying!" said Nell, indignantly. "But did she not give you a note?"

"She was too much upset," said Will, signing to the captain not to let on that they had refused to wait for the note.

"I wonder what it can be," murmured Nell.

She hurried from the room to her father's den, and found him there surrounded by newspapers.

"Is there anything in the *Mirror*, father?" she asked.

"Nothing," said Mr. Meredith, who had made the same answer to this question many hundreds of times, "nothing except depression in the boot trade."

"It can't be that," said Nell.

"Can't be what?"

"Oh, give me the paper," cried the ex-mayor's daughter, impatiently.

She looked hastily up and down it, with an involuntary glance at the births, deaths, and marriages, turned it inside out and outside in, and then exclaimed, "Oh!" Mr. Meredith, who was too

much accustomed to his daughter's impulses to
think that there was much wrong, listened pa-
tiently while she ejaculated, "Horrid!" "What a
shame!" "Oh, I wish I was a man!" and, "Well,
I can't understand it." When she tossed the
paper to the floor, her face was red and her body
trembled with excitement.

"What is it, Nelly?" asked her father.

Whether Miss Abinger cried over the *Mirror*
that day is not to be known, but there were indignant tears in Nell's eyes as she ran upstairs to her
bedroom. Mr. Meredith took up the paper and
examined it carefully at the place where his
daughter had torn it in her anger. What troubled
her seemed to be something in the book notices,
and he concluded that it must be a cruel "slating"
of a novel in one volume called "The Scorn of
Scorns." Mr. Meredith remembered that Nell had
compelled him to read that book and to say that
he liked it.

"That's all," he said to himself, much relieved.

He fancied that Nell, being a girl, was distressed
to see a book she liked called "the sentimental
outpourings of some silly girl who ought to confine
her writing to copy-books." In a woman so much
excitement over nothing seemed quite a natural
thing to Mr. Meredith. The sex had ceased to
surprise him. Having retired from business, Mr.
Meredith now did things slowly as a good way of

passing the time. He had risen to wealth from penury, and counted time by his dining-room chairs, having passed through a cane, a horsehair, and a leather period before arriving at morocco. Mrs. Meredith counted time by the death of her only son.

It may be presumed that Nell would not have locked herself into her bedroom and cried and stamped her feet on an imaginary critic had "The Scorn of Scorns" not interested her more than her father thought. She sat down to write a note to Mary. Then she tore it up, and wrote a letter to Mary's elder brother, beginning with the envelope. She tore this up also, as another idea came into her head. She nodded several times to herself over this idea, as a sign that the more she thought of it the more she liked it. Then, after very nearly forgetting to touch her eyes with something that made them look less red, she returned to the drawing-room.

"Will," she said, "have you seen the new ponies papa gave me on my birthday?"

Will leapt to his feet.

"Come on, Greybrooke," he cried, making for the door.

The captain hesitated.

"Perhaps," said Nell, with a glance at him, "Mr. Greybrooke does not have much interest in horses?"

"Doesn't he, just," said Will; "why—"

"No," said Greybrooke; "but I'll wait here for you, Abinger."

Will was staggered. For a moment the horrible thought passed through his mind that these girls had got hold of the captain. Then he remembered.

"Come on," he said, "Nell won't mind."

But Greybrooke had a delicious notion that the young lady wanted to see him by himself, and Will had to go to the stables alone.

"I won't be long," he said to Greybrooke, apologizing for leaving him alone with a girl. "Don't bother him too much," he whispered to Nell at the door.

As soon as Will had disappeared Nell turned to Greybrooke.

"Mr. Greybrooke," she said, speaking rapidly, in a voice so low that it was a compliment to him in itself, "there is something I should like you to do for me."

The captain flushed with pleasure.

"There is nothing I wouldn't do for you," he stammered.

"I want you," continued Miss Meredith, with a most vindictive look on her face, "to find out for me who wrote a book review in to-day's *Mirror*, and to—to—oh, to thrash him."

"All right," said the captain, rising and looking for his hat.

"Wait a minute," said Nell, glancing at him admiringly. "The book is called 'The Scorn of Scorns,' and it is written by — by a friend of mine. In to-day's *Mirror* it is called the most horrid names, sickly sentimental, not even grammatical, and all that."

"The cads!" cried Greybrooke.

"But the horribly mean wicked thing about it," continued Nell, becoming more and more indignant as she told her story, "is that not two months ago there was a review of the book in the same paper, which said it was the most pathetic and thoughtful and clever tale that had ever been published by an anonymous author!"

"It's the lowest thing I ever heard of," said Greybrooke, "but these newspaper men are all the same."

"No, they're not," said Nell, sharply (Richard Abinger, Esq.'s, only visible means of sustenance was the press), "but they are dreadfully mean, contemptible creatures on the *Mirror* — just reporters, you know."

Greybrooke nodded, though he knew nothing about it.

"The first review," Nell continued, "appeared on the 3rd of October, and I want you to show them both to the editor, and insist upon knowing the name of the writer. After that find the wretch out, and — "

64

"And lick him," said the captain.

His face frightened Nell.

"You won't hit him very hard?" she asked, apprehensively, adding as an afterthought, "Perhaps he is stronger than you."

Greybrooke felt himself in an unfortunate position. He could not boast before Nell, but he wished very keenly that Will was there to boast for him. Most of us have experienced the sensation.

Nell having undertaken to keep Will employed until the captain's return, Greybrooke set off for the *Mirror* office with a look of determination on his face. He went into two shops, the one a news-shop, where he bought a copy of the paper. In the other he asked for a thick stick, having remembered that the elegant cane he carried was better fitted for swinging in the air than for breaking a newspaper man's head. He tried the stick on a paling. Greybrooke felt certain that Miss Meredith was the novelist. That was why he selected so thick a weapon.

He marched into the advertising office, and demanded to see the editor of the *Mirror*.

"'Stairs," said a clerk, with his head in a ledger. He meant upstairs, and the squire of dames took his advice. After wandering for some time in a labyrinth of dark passages, he opened the door of the day composing-room, in which half a dozen silent figures were bending over their cases.

" I want the editor," said Greybrooke, somewhat startled by the sound his voice made in the great room.

" 'Stairs," said one of the figures, meaning downstairs.

Greybrooke, remembering who had sent him here, did not lose heart. He knocked at several doors, and then pushed them open. All the rooms were empty. Then he heard a voice saying —

" Who are you? What do you want?"

Mr. Licquorish was the speaker, and he had been peering at the intruder for some time through a grating in his door. He would not have spoken at all, but he wanted to go into the composing-room, and Greybrooke was in the passage that led to it.

" I don't see you," said the captain; " I want the editor."

" I am the editor," said the voice, " but I can see no one at present except on business."

" I am here on business," said Greybrooke. " I want to thrash one of your staff."

" All the members of my literary staff are engaged at present," said Mr. Licquorish, in a pleasant voice; " which one do you want?"

" I want the low cad who wrote a review of a book called ' The Scorn of Scorns ' in to-day's paper."

" Oh!" said Mr. Licquorish.

" I demand his name," cried Greybrooke.

66

The editor made no answer. He had other things to do than to quarrel with schoolboys. As he could not get out he began a leaderette. The visitor, however, had discovered the editorial door now, and was shaking it violently.

"Why don't you answer me?" he cried.

Mr. Licquorish thought for a moment of calling down the speaking-tube which communicated with the advertisement office, for a clerk to come and take this youth away, but after all he was good-natured. He finished a sentence, and then opened the door. The captain strode in, but refused a chair.

"Are you the author of the book?" the editor asked.

"No," said Greybrooke, "but I am her friend, and I am here to thrash—"

Mr. Licquorish held up his hand to stop the flow of the captain's indignation. He could never understand why the public got so excited over these little matters.

"She is a Silchester lady?" he asked.

Greybrooke did not know how to reply to this. He was not sure whether Nell wanted the author-ship revealed.

"That has nothing to do with the matter," he said. "I want the name of the writer who has libelled her."

"On the press," said Mr. Licquorish, repeating

67

;ome phrases which he kept for such an occasion
as the present, "we have a duty to the public to
perform. When books are sent us for review we
never allow prejudice or private considerations to
warp our judgment. The *Mirror* has in consequence a reputation for honesty that some papers
do not possess. Now I distinctly remember that
this book, 'The Vale of Tears'—"

"'The Scorn of Scorns.'"

"I mean 'The Scorn of Scorns,' was carefully
considered by the expert to whom it was given
for review. Being honestly of opinion that the
treatise—"

"It is a novel."

"That the novel is worthless, we had to say so.
Had it been clever, we should—"

Mr. Licquorish paused, reading in the other's
face that there was something wrong. Greybrooke
had concluded that the editor had forgotten about
the first review.

"Can you show me a copy of the *Mirror*," the
captain asked, "for October 3rd?"

Mr. Licquorish turned to the file, and Greybrooke looked over his shoulder.

"There it is!" cried the captain, indignantly.

They read the original notice together. It said
that, if "The Scorn of Scorns" was written by a
new writer, his next story would be looked for
with great interest. It "could not refrain from

quoting the following exquisitely tender passage."
It found the earlier pages "as refreshing as a spring
morning," and the closing chapters were a triumph
of "the art that conceals art."

"Well, what have you to say to that?" asked
Greybrooke, fiercely.

"A mistake," said the editor, blandly. "Such
things do happen occasionally."

"You shall make reparation for it!"

"Hum," said Mr. Licquorish.

"The insult," cried Greybrooke, "must have
been intentional."

"No. I fancy the authoress must be to blame
for this. Did she send a copy of the work to us?"

"I should think it very unlikely," said Greybrooke, fuming.

"Not at all," said the editor, "especially if she
is a Silchester lady."

"What would make her do that?"

"It generally comes about in this way. The
publishers send a copy of the book to a newspaper,
and owing to pressure on the paper's space no notice appears for some time. The author, who looks
for it daily, thinks that the publishers have neglected their duty, and sends a copy to the office
himself. The editor, forgetful that he has had a
notice of the book lying ready for printing for
months, gives the second copy to another reviewer.
By and by the first review appears, but owing to

an oversight the editor does not take note of it, and after a time, unless his attention is called to the matter, the second review appears also. Probably that is the explanation in this case."

"But such carelessness on a respectable paper is incomprehensible," said the captain.

The editor was looking up his books to see if they shed any light on the affair, but he answered —

"On the contrary, it is an experience known to most newspapers. Ah, I have it!"

Mr. Licquorish read out, "'The Scorn of Scorns,' received September 1st, reviewed October 3rd." Several pages further on he discovered, "'The Scorn of Scorns,' received September 24th, reviewed December 19th."

"You will find," he said, "that this explains it."

"I don't consider the explanation satisfactory," replied the captain, "and I insist, first, upon an apology in the paper, and second, on getting the name of the writer of the second review."

"I am busy this morning," said Mr. Licquorish, opening his door, "and what you ask is absurd. If the authoress can give me her word that she did not send the book and so bring this upon herself, we shall insert a word on the subject, but not otherwise. Good morning."

"Give me the writer's name," cried the captain.

"We make a point of never giving names in that way," said Mr. Licquorish.

"You have not heard the last of this," Greybrooke said from the doorway. "I shall make it my duty to ferret out the coward's name, and — "

"Good morning," Mr. Licquorish repeated.

The captain went thumping down the stairs, and meeting a printer's devil at the bottom, cuffed him soundly because he was part of the *Mirror*.

To his surprise, Miss Meredith's first remark when he returned was —

"Oh, I hope you didn't see him."

She looked at Greybrooke's face, fearing it might be stained with blood, and when he told her the result of his inquiries she seemed pleased rather than otherwise. Nell was soft-hearted after all, and she knew how that second copy of the novel had reached the *Mirror* office.

"I shall find the fellow out, though," said Greybrooke, grasping his cudgel firmly.

"Why, you are as vindictive as if you had written the book yourself," said Nell.

Greybrooke murmured, blushing the while, that an insult to her hurt him more than one offered to himself. Nell opened the eyes of astonishment.

"You don't think I wrote the book?" she asked; then seeing that it was so from his face, added, "Oh no, I'm not clever enough. It was written by — by a friend of mine."

Nell deserves credit for not telling Greybrooke who the friend was, for that was a Secret. But there was reason to believe that she had already divulged it to twelve persons (all in the strictest confidence). When the captain returned she was explaining all about it by letter to Richard Abinger, Esq. Possibly that was why Greybrooke thought she was not nearly so nice to him now as she had been an hour before.

Will was unusually quiet when he and Greybrooke said adieu to the whole family of Merediths. He was burning to know where the captain had been, and also what Nell called him back to say in such a low tone. What she said was —

"Don't say anything about going to the *Mirror* office, Mr. Greybrooke, to Miss Abinger."

The captain turned round to lift his hat, and at the same time expressed involuntarily a wish that Nell could see him punishing loose bowling.

Mrs. Meredith beamed to him.

"There is something very nice," she said to Nell, "about a polite young man."

"Yes," murmured her daughter, "and even if he isn't polite."

CHAPTER V

On the morning before Christmas a murder was committed in Silchester, and in murders there is "lineage." As a consequence, the head reporter attends to them himself. In the *Mirror* office the diary for the day was quickly altered. Kirker set off cheerfully for the scene of the crime, leaving the banquet in the Henry Institute to Tomlinson, who passed on his dinner at Dome Castle to Rob, whose church decorations were taken up by John Milton.

Christmas Eve was coming on in snow when Rob and Walsh, of the *Argus*, set out for Dome Castle. Rob disliked doing dinners at any time, partly because he had not a dress suit. The dinner was an annual one given by Will's father to his tenants, and reporters were asked because the colonel made a speech. His neighbours, when they did likewise, sent reports of their own speeches (which they seemed to like) to the papers; and some of them, having called themselves eloquent and justly popular, scored the compliments out, yet in such a way that the editor would still be able to read them, and print them if he thought fit. Rob did not look forward to Colonel Abinger's reception of him, for they had met some months before, and called each other names.

It was one day soon after Rob reached Silchester. He had gone a-fishing in the Dome and climbed unconsciously into preserved waters. As his creel grew heavier his back straightened; not until he returned home did the scenery impress him. He had just struck a fine fish, when a soldierly-looking man at the top of the steep bank caught sight of him.

"Hie, you sir!" shouted the onlooker. Whir went the line — there is no music like it. Rob was knee-deep in water. "You fellow!" cried the other, brandishing his cane, "are you aware that this water is preserved?" Rob had no time for talk. The colonel sought to attract his attention by flinging a pebble. "Don't do that," cried Rob, fiercely.

Away went the fish. Away went Rob after it. Colonel Abinger's face was red as he clambered down the bank. "I shall prosecute you," he shouted. "He's gone to the bottom; fling in a stone!" cried Rob. Just then the fish showed its yellow belly and darted off again. Rob let out more line. "No, no," shouted the colonel, who fished himself, "you lose him if he gets to the other side; strike, man, strike!" The line tightened, the rod bent — a glorious sight. "Force him up stream," cried the colonel, rolling over boulders to assist. "Now, you have him. Bring him in. Where is your landing net?" "I haven't one," cried Rob; "take him in your hands." The colonel stooped to grasp the fish and missed it. "Bungler!" screamed Rob. This was too much. "Give me your name and address," said Colonel Abinger, rising to his feet; "you are a poacher." Rob paid no attention. There was a struggle. Rob did not realize that he had pushed his assailant over a rock until the fish was landed. Then he apologized, offered all his fish in lieu of his name and address, retired coolly so long as the furious soldier was in sight, and as soon as he turned a corner disappeared rapidly. He could not feel that this was the best introduction to the man with whom he was now on his way to dine.

The reporter whose long strides made Walsh trot as they hurried to Dome Castle, was not quite the Rob of three months before. Now he knew how a third-rate newspaper is conducted, and the capacity for wonder had gone from him. He was in danger of thinking that the journalist's art is to write readably, authoritatively, and always in three paragraphs on a subject he knows nothing about. Rob had written many leaders, and followed readers through the streets wondering if they liked them. Once he had gone with three others to report a bishop's sermon. A curate appeared instead, and when the reporters saw him they shut their note-books and marched blandly out of the cathedral. A public speaker had tried to bribe Rob with two half-crowns, and it is still told in Silchester how the wrathful Scotsman tore his benefactor out of the carriage he had just stepped into, and, lifting him on high, looked around to consider against which stone wall he should hurl him. He had discovered that on the first of the month Mr. Licquorish could not help respecting his staff, because on that day he paid them. Socially Rob had acquired little. Protheroe had introduced him to a pleasant family, but he had sat silent in a corner, and they told the sub-editor not to bring him back. Most of the literary staff were youths trying to be Bohemians, who liked to feel themselves sinking, and they never scaled the reserve which walled Rob round. He had taken a sitting, however, in the Scotch church, to the bewilderment of the minister, who said, "But I thought you were a reporter?" as if there must be a mistake somewhere.

Walsh could tell Rob little of Colonel Abinger. He was a brave soldier, and for many years had been a widower. His elder son was a barrister in London, whom Silchester had almost forgotten, and Walsh fancied there was some story about the daughter's being engaged to a baronet. There was also a boy, who had the other day brought the captain of his school to a Silchester football ground to show the club how to take a drop-kick.

"Does the colonel fish?" asked Rob, who would, however, have preferred to know if the colonel had a good memory for faces.

"He is a famous angler," said Walsh; "indeed, I have been told that his bursts of passion are over in five minutes, except when he catches a poacher."

Rob winced, for Walsh did not know of the fishing episode.

"His temper," continued Walsh, "is such that his male servants are said never to know whether he will give them a shilling or a whirl of his cane — until they get it. The gardener takes a look at him from behind a tree before venturing to address him. I suppose his poverty is at the bottom of it, for the estate is mortgaged heavily, and he has had to cut down trees, and even to sell his horses. The tenants seem to like him, though, and if they dared they would tell him not to think himself bound to give them this annual dinner. There are numberless stories of his fierce temper, and as many of his extravagant kindness. According to his servants, he once emptied his pocket to a beggar at a railway station, and then discovered that he had no money for his own ticket. As for the ne'er-do-weels, their importuning makes him rage, but they know he will fling them something in the end if they expose their rags sufficiently."

"So," said Rob, who did not want to like the colonel, "he would not trouble about them if they kept their misery to themselves. That kind of man is more likely to be a philanthropist in your country than in mine."

"Keep that for a Burns dinner," suggested Walsh.

Rob heard now how Tomlinson came to be nicknamed Umbrage.

"He was sub-editing one night," Walsh explained, "during the time of an African war, and things were going so smoothly that he and Penny were chatting amicably together about the advantage of having a few Latin phrases in a leader, such as *dolce far niente*, or *cela va sans dire* — "

"I can believe that," said Rob, "of Penny certainly."

"Well, in the middle of the discussion an important war telegram arrived, to the not unnatural disgust of both. As is often the case, the message was misspelt, and barely decipherable, and one part of it puzzled Tomlinson a good deal. It read: 'Zulus have taken Umbrage; English forces had to retreat.' Tomlinson searched the map in vain for Umbrage, which the Zulus had taken;

and Penny, being in a hurry, was sure it was a fortress. So they risked it, and next morning the chief lines in the *Mirror* contents bill were : 'LATEST NEWS OF THE WAR; CAPTURE OF UMBRAGE BY THE ZULUS.' "

By this time the reporters had passed into the grounds of the castle, and, being late, were hurrying up the grand avenue. It was the hour and the season when night comes on so sharply, that its shadow may be seen trailing the earth as a breeze runs along a field of corn. Heard from a height the roar of the Dome among rocks might have been the rustle of the surrounding trees in June ; so men and women who grow old together sometimes lend each other a voice. Walsh, seeing his opportunity in Rob's silence, began to speak of himself. He told how his first press-work had been a series of letters he had written when at school, and contributed to a local paper under the signatures of " Paterfamilias " and " An Indignant Ratepayer." Rob scarcely heard. The bare romantic scenery impressed him, and the snow in his face was like a whiff of Thrums. He was dreaming, but not of the reception he might get at the castle, when the clatter of horses awoke him.

" There is a machine behind us," he said, though he would have written trap.

A brougham lumbered into sight. As its lamps flashed on the pedestrians, the coachman jerked his

79

horses to the side, and Rob had a glimpse of the carriage's occupant. The brougham stopped.

"I beg your pardon," said the traveller, opening his window, and addressing Rob, "but in the darkness I mistook you for Colonel Abinger."

"We are on our way to the castle," said Walsh, stepping forward.

"Ah, then," said the stranger, "perhaps you will give me your company for the short distance we have still to go?"

There was a fine courtesy in his manner that made the reporters feel their own deficiencies, yet Rob thought the stranger repented his offer as soon as it was made. Walsh had his hand on the door, but Rob said—

"We are going to Dome Castle as reporters."

"Oh!" said the stranger. Then he bowed graciously, and pulled up the window. The carriage rumbled on, leaving the reporters looking at each other. Rob laughed. For the first time in his life the advantage a handsome man has over a plain one had struck him. He had only once seen such a face before, and that was in marble in the Silchester Art Museum. This man looked thirty years of age, but there was not a line on his broad, white brow. The face was magnificently classic, from the strong Roman nose to the firm chin. The eyes, too beautiful almost for his sex, were brown and wistful, of the kind that droop in disappointment oftener than they blaze with anger. All the hair on his face was a heavy drooping moustache that almost hid his mouth.

Walsh shook his fist at this insult to the Press. "It is the baronet I spoke of to you," he said. "I forget who he is; indeed, I rather think he travelled *incognito* when he was here last. I don't understand what he is doing here."

"Why, I should say this is just the place where he would be if he is to marry Miss Abinger."

"That was an old story," said Walsh. "If there ever was an engagement it was broken off. Besides, if he had been expected we should have known of it at the *Argus*."

Walsh was right. Sir Clement Dowton was not expected at Dome Castle, and, like Rob, he was not even certain that he would be welcome. As he drew near his destination his hands fidgetted with the window strap, yet there was an unaccountable twinkle in his eye. Had there been any onlookers they would have been surprised to see that all at once the baronet's sense of humour seemed to overcome his fears, and instead of quaking he laughed heartily. Sir Clement was evidently one of the men who carry their joke about with them.

This unexpected guest did Rob one good turn. When the colonel saw Sir Clement he hesitated for a moment as if not certain how to greet him.

Then the baronet, who was effusive, murmured
that he had something to say to him, and Colonel
Abinger's face cleared. He did Sir Clement the
unusual honour of accompanying him upstairs
himself, and so Rob got the seat assigned to him
at the dinner-table without having to meet his host
in the face. The butler marched him down a
long table with a twist in it, and placed him
under arrest, as it were, in a chair from which he
saw only a few of the company. The dinner had
already begun, but the first thing he realized as he
took his seat was that there was a lady on each
side of him, and a table-napkin in front. He was
not sure if he was expected to address the ladies,
and he was still less certain about the table-napkin.
Of such things he had read, and he had even tried
to be prepared for them. Rob looked nervously
at the napkin, and then took a covert glance along
the table. There was not a napkin in sight except
one which a farmer had tied round his neck.
Rob's fingers wanted to leave the napkin alone,
but by an effort he forced them toward it. All
this time his face was a blank, but the internal
struggle was sharp. He took hold of the napkin,
however, and spread it on his knees. It fell to the
floor immediately afterwards, but he disregarded that.
It was no longer staring at him from the table, and
with a heavy sigh of relief he began to feel more at
ease. There is nothing like burying our bogies.

ROB MARCHES TO HIS FATE

His position prevented Rob's seeing either the colonel at the head of the table or Miss Abinger at the foot of it, and even Walsh was hidden from view. But his right-hand neighbour was a local doctor's wife, whom the colonel had wanted to honour without honouring too much, and she gave him some information. Rob was relieved to hear her address him, and she was interested in a tame Scotsman.

"I was once in the far north myself," she said, "as far as Orkney. We were nearly drowned in crossing that dreadful sea between it and the mainland. The Solway Firth, is it?"

Rob thought for a moment of explaining what sea it is, and then he thought, why should he?

"Yes, the Solway Firth," he said.

"It was rather an undertaking," she pursued, "but though we were among the mountains for days, we never encountered any of those robber chieftains one reads about — caterans I think you call them?"

"You were very lucky," said Rob.

"Were we not? But, you know, we took such precautions. There was quite a party of us, including my father, who has travelled a great deal, and all the gentlemen wore kilts. My father said it was always prudent to do in Rome as the Romans do."

"I have no doubt," said Rob, "that in that way

you escaped the caterans. They are very open to flattery."

"So my father said. We also found that we could make ourselves understood by saying, 'whatever' and remembering to call the men 'she' and the women 'he.' What a funny custom that is!"

"We can't get out of it," said Rob.

"There is one thing," the lady continued, "that you can tell me. I have been told that in winter the wild boars take refuge in the streets of Inverness, and that there are sometimes very exciting hunts after them?"

"That is only when they run away with children," Rob explained. "Then the natives go out in large bodies and shoot them with claymores. It is a most exciting scene."

When the doctor's wife learned that this was Rob's first visit to the castle, she told him at once that she was there frequently. It escaped his notice that she paused here and awaited the effect. She was not given to pausing.

"My husband," she said, "attended on Lady Louisa during her last illness — quite ten years ago. I was married very young," she added, hurriedly.

Rob was very nearly saying he saw that. The words were in his mouth, when he hesitated, reflecting that it was not worth while. This is only noticeable as showing that he missed his first compliment.

"Lady Louisa?" he repeated instead.

"Oh, yes, the colonel married one of Lord Tarlington's daughters. There were seven of them, you know, and no sons, and when the youngest was born it was said that a friend of his lordship sent him a copy of Wordsworth, with the page turned down at the poem, 'We are Seven' — a lady friend, I believe."

"Is Miss Abinger like the colonel?" asked Rob, who had heard it said that she was beautiful, and could not help taking an interest in her in consequence.

"You have not seen Miss Abinger?" asked the doctor's wife. "Ah, you came late, and that vulgar-looking farmer hides her altogether. She is a lovely girl, but — "

Rob's companion pursed her lips.

"She is so cold and proud," she added.

"As proud as her father?" Rob asked, aghast.

"Oh, the colonel is humility itself beside her. He freezes at times, but she never thaws."

Rob sighed involuntarily. He was not aware that his acquaintances spoke in a similar way of him. His eyes wandered up the table till they rested of their own accord on a pretty girl in blue, At that moment she was telling Greybrooke that he could call her Nell, because "Miss" Meredith sounded like a reproach.

The reporter looked at Nell with satisfaction,

and the doctor's wife followed his thoughts so accurately that, before she could check herself, she said, " Do you think so ? "

Then Rob started, which confused both of them, and for the remainder of the dinner the loquacious lady seemed to take less interest in him, he could not understand why. Flung upon his own re sources, he remembered that he had not spoken to the lady on his other side. Had Rob only known it, she felt much more uncomfortable in that great dining-room than he did. No one was speaking to her, and she passed the time between the courses breaking her bread to pieces and eating it slowly crumb by crumb. Rob thought of something to say to her, but when he tried the words over in his own mind they seemed so little worth saying that he had to think again. He found himself counting the crumbs, and then it struck him that he might ask her if she would like any salt. He did so, but she thought he asked for salt, and passed the salt-cellar to him, whereupon Rob, as the simplest way to get out of it, helped himself to more salt, though he did not need it. The intercourse thus auspiciously begun, went no further, and they never met again. It might have been a romance.

The colonel had not quite finished his speech, which was to the effect that so long as his tenants looked up to him as some one superior to themselves they would find him an indulgent landlord, when the tread of feet was heard outside, and then the music of the waits. The colonel frowned and raised his voice, but his guests caught themselves tittering, and read their host's rage in his darkening face. Forgetting that the waits were there by his own invitation, he signed to James, the butler, to rush out and mow them down. James did not interpret the message so, but for the moment it was what his master meant.

While the colonel was hesitating whether to go on, Rob saw Nell nod encouragingly to Greybrooke. He left his seat, and before any one knew what he was about, had flung open one of the windows. The room filled at once with music, and, as if by common consent, the table was deserted. Will opened the remaining windows, and the waits, who had been singing to shadows on the white blinds, all at once found a crowded audience. Rob hardly realized what it meant, for he had never heard the waits before.

It was a scene that would have silenced a schoolgirl. The night was so clear, that beyond the lawn where the singers were grouped the brittle trees showed in every twig. No snow was falling, and so monotonous was the break of the river, that the ear would only have noticed it had it stopped. The moon stood overhead like a frozen round of snow.

Looking over the heads of those who had gathered at one of the windows, Rob saw first Will Abinger and then the form of a girl cross to the singers. Some one followed her with a cloak. From the French windows steps dropped to the lawn. A lady beside Rob shivered and retired to the fireside, but Nell whispered to Greybrooke that she must run after Mary. Several others followed her down the steps.

Rob, looking round for Walsh, saw him in conversation with the colonel. Probably he was taking down the remainder of the speech. Then a lady's voice said, "Who is that magnificent young man?"

The sentence ended "with the hob-nailed boots," and the reference was to Rob, but he only caught the first words. He thought the baronet was spoken of, and suddenly remembered that he had not appeared at the dinner-table. As Sir Clement entered the room at that moment in evening dress, making most of those who surrounded him look mean by comparison, Rob never learned who the magnificent young man was.

Sir Clement's entrance was something of a sensation, and Rob saw several ladies raise their eyebrows. All seemed to know him by name, and some personally. The baronet's nervousness had evidently passed away, for he bowed and smiled to every one, claiming some burly farmers as old acquaintances though he had never seen them before.

His host and he seemed already on the most cordial terms, but the colonel was one of the few persons in the room who was not looking for Miss Abinger. At last Sir Clement asked for her.

" I believe," said some one in answer to the colonel's inquiring glance round the room, " that Miss Abinger is speaking with the waits."

" Perhaps I shall see her," said Dowton, stepping out at one of the windows.

Colonel Abinger followed him to the window, but no further, and at that moment a tall figure on the snowy lawn crossed his line of vision. It was Rob, who, not knowing what to do with himself, had wandered into the open. His back was toward the colonel, and something in his walk recalled to that choleric officer the angler whom he had encountered on the Dome.

" That is the man — I was sure I knew the face," said Colonel Abinger. He spoke in a whisper to himself, but his hands closed with a snap.

Unconscious of all this, Rob strolled on till he found a path that took him round the castle. Suddenly he caught sight of a blue dress, and at the same moment a girl's voice exclaimed, " Oh, I am afraid it is lost!"

The speaker bent, as if to look for something in the snow, and Rob blundered up to her. " If you have lost anything," he said, "perhaps I can find it."

Rob had matches in his pocket, and he struck

one of them. Then, to his surprise, he noticed that Nell was not alone. Greybrooke was with her, and he was looking foolish.

"Thank you very much," said Nell, sweetly; "it is a — a bracelet."

Rob went down on his knees to look for the bracelet, but it surprised him a little that Greybrooke did not follow his example. If he had looked up, he would have seen that the captain was gazing at Nell in amazement.

"I am afraid it is lost," Nell repeated, "or perhaps I dropped it in the dining-room."

Greybrooke's wonder was now lost in a grin, for Nell had lost nothing, unless perhaps for the moment her sense of what was fit and proper. The captain had followed her on to the lawn, and persuaded her to come and look down upon the river from the top of the cliff. She had done so, she told herself, because he was a boy; but he had wanted her to do it because she was a woman. On the very spot where Richard Abinger, barrister-at-law, had said something to her that Nell would never forget, the captain had presumptuously kissed her hand, and Nell had allowed him, because after all it was soon over. It was at that very moment that Rob came in sight, and Nell thought she was justified in deceiving him. Rob would have remained a long time on the snow if she had not had a heart.

∞

" Yes, I believe I did drop it in the dining-room," said Nell, in such a tone of conviction that Rob rose to his feet. His knees were white in her service, and Nell felt that she liked this young man.

" I am so sorry to have troubled you, Mr. — Mr. — " began the young lady.

" My name is Angus," said Rob; " I am a reporter on the *Silchester Mirror.*"

Greybrooke started, and Nell drew back in horror, but the next second she was smiling. Rob thought it was kindliness that made her do it, but it was really a smile of triumph. She felt that she was on the point of making a discovery at last. Greybrooke would have blurted out a question, but Nell stopped him.

" Get me a wrap of some kind, Mr. Greybrooke," she said, with such sweet imperiousness that the captain went without a word. Half way he stopped to call himself a fool, for he had remembered all at once about Raleigh and his cloak, and seen how he might have adapted that incident to his advantage by offering to put his own coat round Nell's shoulders.

It was well that Greybrooke did not look back, for he would have seen Miss Meredith take Rob's arm — which made Rob start — and lead him in the direction in which Miss Abinger was supposed to have gone.

" The literary life must be delightful," said artful Nell, looking up into her companion's face.

Rob appreciated the flattery, but his pride made him say that the literary life was not the reporter's.

"I always read the *Mirror*," continued Nell, on whom the moon was having a bad effect to-night, "and often I wonder who writes the articles. There was a book-review in it a few days ago that I — I liked very much."

"Do you remember what the book was?" asked Rob, jumping into the pit.

"Let me see," said Nell, putting her head to the side, "it was — yes, it was a novel called — called 'The Scorn of Scorns.'"

Rob's good angel was very near him at that moment, but not near enough to put her palm over his mouth.

"That review was mine," said Rob, with un-called-for satisfaction.

"Was it?" cried his companion, pulling away her arm viciously.

The path had taken them to the top of the pile of rocks, from which it is a sheer descent of a hundred feet to the Dome. At this point the river is joined by a smaller, but not less noisy stream, which rushes at it at right angles. Two of the castle walls rise up here as if part of the cliff, and though the walk goes round them, they seem to the angler looking up from the opposite side of the Dome to be part of the rock. From the windows that look to the west and north one can see down into the black waters, and hear the Ferret, as the smaller stream is called, fling itself over jagged boulders into the Dome.

The ravine coming upon him suddenly, took away Rob's breath, and he hardly felt Nell snatch away her arm. She stood back, undecided what to do for a moment, and they were separated by a few yards. Then Rob heard a man's voice, soft and low, but passionate. He knew it to be Sir Clement Dowton's, though he lost the words. A girl's voice answered, however, a voice so exquisitely modulated, so clear and pure, that Rob trembled with delight in it. This is what it said —

"No, Sir Clement Dowton, I bear you no ill-will, but I do not love you. Years ago I made an idol and worshipped it, because I knew no better, but I am a foolish girl no longer, and I know now that it was a thing of clay."

To Rob's amazement he found himself murmuring these words even before they were spoken. He seemed to know them so well, that had the speaker missed anything, he could have put her right. It was not sympathy that worked this marvel. He had read all this before, or something very like it, in "The Scorn of Scorns."

Nell, too, heard the voice, but did not catch the words. She ran forward, and as she reached Rob, a tall girl in white, with a dark hood over her head, pushed aside a bush and came into view.

"Mary," cried Miss Meredith, "this gentleman
here is the person who wrote *that* in the *Mirror*.
Let me introduce you to him, Mr. Angus, Miss — "
and then Nell shrank back in amazement, as she
saw who was with her friend.

"Sir Clement Dowton!" she exclaimed.

Rob, however, did not hear her, nor see the
baronet, for looking up with a guilty feeling at
his heart, his eyes met Mary Abinger.

CHAPTER VI

THE ONE WOMAN

DAYBREAK on the following morning found the gas blazing in Rob's lodgings. Rob was seated in an armchair, his feet on the cold hearth. "The Scorn of Scorns" lay on the mantlepiece carefully done up in brown paper, lest a speck of dust should fall on it, and he had been staring at the ribs of the fireplace for the last three hours without seeing them. He had not thought of the gas. His bed was unslept on. His damp boots had dried on his feet. He did not feel cold. All night he had sat there, a man mesmerized. For the only time in his life he had forgotten to wind up his watch.

At times his lips moved as if he were speaking to himself, and a smile lit up his face. Then a change of mood came, and he beat the fender with his feet till the fire-irons rattled. Thinking over these remarks brought the rapture to his face :

"How do you do, Mr. Angus?"

"You must not take to heart what Miss Meredith said."

"Please don't say any more about it. I am

95

quite sure you gave your honest opinion about my book."

" I am so glad you think this like Scotland, because, of course, that is the highest compliment a Scotsman can pay."

" Good night, Mr. Angus."

That was all she had said to him, but the more Rob thought over her remarks the more he liked them. It was not so much the words themselves that thrilled him as the way they were said. Other people had asked, " How do you do, Mr. Angus? " without making an impression, but her greeting was a revelation of character, for it showed that though she knew who he was she wanted to put him at his ease. This is a delightful attribute in a woman, and worth thinking about.

Just before Miss Abinger said, " How do you do, Mr. Angus? " Rob had realized what people meant by calling her proud. She was holding her head very high as she appeared in the path, and when Nell told her who Rob was she flushed. He looked hopelessly at her, bereft of speech, as he saw a tear glisten on her eyelid; and as their eyes met she read into the agony that he was suffering because he had hurt her. It was then that Mary made that memorable observation, " How do you do, Mr. Angus? "

They turned toward the castle doors, Nell and the baronet in front, and Rob blurted out some

self-reproaches in sentences that had neither beginning nor end. Mary had told him not to take it so terribly to heart, but her voice trembled a little, for this had been a night of incident to her. Rob knew that it was for his sake she had checked that tear, and as he sat in his lodgings through the night he saw that she had put aside her own troubles to lessen his. When he thought of that he drew a great breath. The next moment his whole body shuddered to think what a brute he had been, and then she seemed to touch his elbow again, and he half rose from his chair in a transport.

As soon as he reached his lodgings Rob had taken up "The Scorn of Scorns," which he had not yet returned to Mr. Licquorish, and re-read it in a daze. There were things in it so beautiful now that they caught in his throat and stopped his reading; they took him so far into the thoughts of a girl that to go further seemed like eavesdropping. When he read it first "The Scorn of Scorns" had been written in a tongue Rob did not know, but now he had the key in his hands. There is a universal language that comes upon young people suddenly, and enables an English girl, for instance, to understand what a Chinaman means when he looks twice at her. Rob had mastered it so suddenly that he was only its slave at present. His horse had run away with him.

Had the critic of "The Scorn of Scorns" been

a bald-headed man with two chins, who did not know the authoress, he would have smiled at the severity with which she took perfidious man to task, and written an indulgent criticism without reading beyond the second chapter. If he had been her father he would have laughed a good deal at her heroics, but now and again they would have touched him, and he would have locked the book away in his desk, seeing no particular cleverness in it, but feeling proud of his daughter. It would have brought such thoughts to him about his wife as suddenly fill a man with tenderness — thoughts he seldom gives expression to, though she would like to hear them.

Rob, however, drank in the book, his brain filled with the writer of it. It was about a young girl who had given her heart to a stranger, and one day when she was full of the joy of his love he had disappeared. She waited wondering, fearing, and then her heart broke, and her only desire was to die. No one could account for the change that came over her, for she was proud, and her relatives were not sympathetic. She had no mother to go to, and her father could not have understood. She became listless, and though she smiled and talked to all, when she went to her solitary bed-chamber she turned her face in silence to the wall. Then a fever came to her, and after that she had to be taken to the continent. What shook her listless-

ness was an accident to her father. It was feared that he was on his deathbed, and as she nursed him she saw that her life had been a selfish one. From that moment she resolved if he got better (Is it not terrible this that the best of us try to make terms with God?) to devote her life to him, and to lead a nobler existence among the poor and suffering ones at home. The sudden death of a relative who was not a good man frightened her so much that she became ill again, and now she was so fearful of being untruthful that she could not make a statement of fact without adding, " I think so," under her breath. She let people take advantage of her lest she should be taking advantage of them, and when she passed a cripple on the road she walked very slowly so that he should not feel his infirmity.

Years afterwards she saw the man who had pretended to love her and then ridden away. He said that he could explain everything to her, and that he loved her still; but she drew herself up, and with a look of ineffable scorn told him that she no longer loved him. When they first met, she said, she had been little more than a child, and so she had made an idol of him. But long since the idol had crumbled to pieces, and now she knew that she had worshipped a thing of clay. She wished him well, but she no longer loved him. As Lord Caltonbridge listened he knew that she spoke the truth, and his eyes drooped before her dignified but contemptuous gaze. Then, concludes the author, dwelling upon this little triumph with a satisfaction that hardly suggests a heart broken beyond mending, he turned upon his heel, at last realizing what he was; and, feeling smaller and meaner than had been his wont, left the Grange for the second and last time.

How much of this might be fiction, Rob was not in a mind to puzzle over. It seemed to him that the soul of a pure-minded girl had been laid bare to him. To look was almost a desecration, and yet it was there whichever way he turned. A great longing rose in his heart to see Mary Abinger again and tell her what he thought of himself now. He rose and paced the floor, and the words he could not speak last night came to his lips in a torrent. Like many men who live much alone Rob often held imaginary conversations with persons far distant, and he denounced himself to this girl a score of times as he paced back and forwards. Always she looked at him in reply with that wonderful smile which had pleaded with him not to be unhappy on her account. Horrible fears laid hold of him that after the guests had departed she had gone to her room and wept. That villain Sir Clement had doubtless left the castle for the second and last time, " feeling smaller and meaner than had been his wont " (Rob clenched his fists

at the thought of him), but how could he dare to
rage at the baronet when he had been as great a
scoundrel himself? Rob looked about him for
his hat; a power not to be resisted was drawing
him back to Dome Castle.

He heard the clatter of crockery in the kitchen,
as he opened his door, and it recalled him to him
self. At that moment it flashed upon him that he
had forgotten to write any notice of Colonel Abinger's speech. He had neglected the office and
come straight home. At any other time this
would have startled him, but now it seemed the
merest trifle. It passed for the moment from his
mind, and its place was taken by the remembrance
that his boots were muddy and his coat soaking.
For the first time in his life the seriousness of going out with his hair unbrushed came home to
him. He had hitherto been content to do little
more than fling a comb at it once a day. Rob returned to his room, and, crossing to the mirror,
looked anxiously into it to see what he was like.
He took off his coat and brushed it vigorously.

Having laved his face, he opened his box and
produced from it two neckties, which he looked at
for a long time before he could make up his
mind which to wear. Then he changed his boots.
When he had brushed his hat he remembered with
anxiety some one on the *Mirror's* having asked
him why he wore it so far back on his head. He

tilted it forward, and carefully examined the effect in the looking-glass. Then, forgetful that the sounds from the kitchen betokened the approach of breakfast, he hurried out of the house. It was a frosty morning, and already the streets were alive, but Rob looked at no one. For women in the abstract he now felt an unconscious pity, because they were all so very unlike Mary Abinger. He had grown so much in the night that the Rob Angus of the day before seemed but an acquaintance of his youth.

He was inside the grounds of Dome Castle again before he realized that he had no longer a right to be there. By fits and starts he remembered not to soil his boots. He might have been stopped at the lodge, but at present it had no tenant. A year before, Colonel Abinger had realized that he could not keep both a horse and a lodge-keeper, and that he could keep neither if his daughter did not part with her maid. He yielded to Miss Abinger's entreaties, and kept the horse.

Rob went on at a swinging pace till he turned an abrupt corner of the walk and saw Dome Castle standing up before him. Then he started, and turned back hastily. This was not owing to his remembering that he was trespassing, but because he had seen a young lady coming down the steps. Rob had walked five miles without his breakfast to talk to Miss Abinger, but as soon as he saw

her he fled. When he came to himself he was so
fearful of her seeing him, that he hurried behind a
tree, where he had the appearance of a burglar.

Mary Abinger came quickly up the avenue,
unconscious that she was watched, and Rob discovered in a moment that after all the prettiest
thing about her was the way she walked. She carried a little basket in her hand, and her dress was
a blending of brown and yellow, with a great deal
of fur about the throat. Rob, however, did not
take the dress into account until she had passed
him, when, no longer able to see her face, he gazed
with delight after her.

Had Rob been a lady he would probably have
come to the conclusion that the reason why Miss
Abinger wore all that fur instead of a jacket was
because she knew it became her better. Perhaps it
was. Even though a young lady has the satisfaction of feeling that her heart is now adamant, that
is no excuse for her dressing badly. Rob's opinion
was that it would matter very little what she wore
because some pictures look lovely in any frame,
but that was a point on which he and Miss Abinger always differed. Only after long consideration had she come to the conclusion that the
hat she was now wearing was undoubtedly the
shape that suited her best, and even yet she was
ready to spend time in thinking about other shapes.
What would have seemed even more surprising to

Rob was that she had made up her mind that one side of her face was better than the other side.

No mere man, however, could ever have told which was the better side of Miss Abinger's face. It was a face to stir the conscience of a good man, and make unworthy men keep their distance, for it spoke first of purity, which can never be present anywhere without being felt. All men are born with a craving to find it, and they never look for it but among women. The strength of the craving is the measure of any man's capacity to love, and without it love on his side would be impossible.

Mary Abinger was fragile because she was so sensitive. She carried everywhere a fear to hurt the feelings of others, that was a bodkin at her heart. Men and women in general prefer to give and take. The keenness with which she felt necessitated the garment of reserve, which those who did not need it for themselves considered pride. Her weakness called for something to wrap it up. There were times when it pleased her to know that the disguise was effective, but not when it deceived persons she admired. The cynicism of "The Scorn of Scorns" was as much a cloak as her coldness, for she had an exquisite love of what is good and fine in life that idealized into heroes persons she knew or heard of as having a virtue. It would have been cruel to her to say that there are no heroes. When she found how little of the heroic there was in Sir Clement Dowton she told herself that there are none, and sometimes other persons had made her repeat this since. She seldom reasoned about things, however, unless her feelings had been wounded, and soon again she was dreaming of the heroic. Heroes are people to love, and Mary's idea of what love must be would have frightened some persons from loving her. With most men affection for a woman is fed on her regard for them. Greatness in love is no more common than greatness in leading armies. Only the hundredth man does not prefer to dally where woman is easiest to win; most finding the maids of honour a satisfactory substitute for the princess. So the boy in the street prefers two poor apples to a sound one. It may be the secret of England's greatness.

On this Christmas Day Mary Abinger came up the walk rapidly, scorning herself for ever having admired Sir Clement Dowton. She did everything in the superlative degree, and so rather wondered that a thunderbolt was not sent direct from above to kill him — as if there were thunderbolts for every one. If we got our deserts most of us would be knocked on the head with a broomstick.

When she was out of sight, Rob's courage returned, and he remembered that he was there in the hope of speaking to her. He hurried up the walk after her, but when he neared her he fell back in alarm. His heart was beating violently. He asked himself in a quaver what it was that he had arranged to say first.

In her little basket Mary had Christmas presents for a few people, inhabitants of a knot of houses not far distant from the castle gates. They were her father's tenants, and he rather enjoyed their being unable to pay much rent, it made them so dependent. Had Rob seen how she was received in some of these cottages, how she sat talking merrily with one bed-ridden old woman whom cheerfulness kept alive, and not only gave a disabled veteran a packet of tobacco, but filled his pipe for him, so that he gallantly said he was reluctant to smoke it (trust an old man for gallantry), and even ate pieces of strange cakes to please her hostesses, he would often have thought of it afterwards. However, it would have been unnecessary prodigality to show him that, for his mind was filled with the incomparable manner in which she knocked at doors and smiled when she came out. Once she dropped her basket, and he could remember nothing so exquisite as her way of picking it up.

Rob lurked behind trees and peered round hedges, watching Miss Abinger go from one house to another, but he could not shake himself free of the fear that all the word had its eye on him.

Hitherto not his honesty but its bluntness had told against him (the honesty of a good many persons is only stupidity asserting itself), and now he had not the courage to be honest. When any way- farers approached he whistled to the fields as if he had lost a dog in them, or walked smartly eastward (until he got round a corner) like one who was in à hurry to reach Silchester. He looked covertly at the few persons who passed him, to see if they were looking at him. A solitary crow fluttered into the air from behind a wall, and Rob started. In a night he had become self-conscious.

At last Mary turned homewards, with the sun in her face. Rob was moving toward the hamlet when he saw her, and in spite of himself he came to a dead stop. He knew that if she passed inside the gates of the castle his last chance of speaking to her was gone; but it was not that which made him keep his ground. He was shaking as the thin boards used to do when they shot past his circular saw. His mind, in short, had run away and left him.

On other occasions Mary would not have thought of doing more than bow to Rob, but he had Christ- mas Day in his favour, and she smiled.

" A happy Christmas to you, Mr. Angus," she said, holding out her hand.

It was then that Rob lifted his hat, and overcame his upbringing. His unaccustomed fingers insisted on lifting it in such a cautious way that, in a court of law, it could have been argued that he was only planting it more firmly on his head. He did not do it well, but he did it. Some men would have succumbed altogether on realizing so sharply that it is not women who are terrible, but a woman. Here is a clear case in which the part is greater than the whole.

Rob would have liked to wish Miss Abinger a happy Christmas too, but the words would not form, and had she chosen she could have left him looking very foolish. But Mary had blushed slightly when she caught sight of Rob standing helplessly in the middle of the road, and this meant that she understood what he was doing there. A girl can overlook a great deal in a man who admires her. She feels happier. It increases her self-respect. So Miss Abinger told him that, if the frost held, the snow would soon harden, but if a thaw came it would melt; and then Rob tore out of himself the words that tended to slip back as they reached his tongue.

" I don't know how I could have done it," he said feebly, beginning at the end of what he had meant to say. There he stuck again.

Mary knew what he spoke of, and her pale face coloured. She shrank from talking of " The Scorn of Scorns."

" Please don't let that trouble you," she said, with

an effort. "I was really only a schoolgirl when I wrote it, and Miss Meredith got it printed recently as a birthday surprise for me. I assure you I would never have thought of publishing it myself for — for people to read. Schoolgirls, you know, Mr. Angus, are full of such silly sentiment."

A breeze of indignation shook "No, No!" out of Rob, but Mary did not heed.

"I know better now," she said; "indeed, not even you, the hardest of my critics, sees more clearly than I the — the childishness of the book."

Miss Abinger's voice faltered a very little, and Rob's sufferings allowed him to break out.

"No," he said, with a look of appeal in his eyes that were as grey as hers, "it was a madness that let me write like that. 'The Scorn of Scorns' is the most beautiful, the tenderest—" He stuck once more. Miss Abinger could have helped him again, but she did not. Perhaps she wanted him to go on. He could not do so, but he repeated what he had said already, which may have been the next best thing to do.

"You do surprise me now, Mr. Angus," said Mary, light-hearted all at once, "for you know you scarcely wrote like that."

"Ah, but I have read the book since I saw you," Rob blurted out, "and that has made such a difference."

A wiser man might have said a more foolish

thing. Mary looked up smiling. Her curiosity was aroused, and at once she became merciless. Hitherto she had only tried to be kind to Rob, but now she wanted to be kind to herself.

"You can hardly have re-read my story since last night," she said, shaking her fair head demurely.

"I read it all through the night," exclaimed Rob, in such a tone that Mary started. She had no desire to change the conversation, however; she did not start so much as that.

"But you had to write papa's speech?" she said.

"I forgot to do it," Rob answered, awkwardly. His heart sank, for he saw that here was another cause he had given Miss Abinger to dislike him. Possibly he was wrong. There may be extenuating circumstances that will enable the best of daughters to overlook an affront to her father's speeches.

"But it was in the *Mirror* I read it," said Mary.

"Was it?" said Rob, considerably relieved. How it could have got there was less of a mystery to him than to her, for Protheroe had sub-edited so many speeches to tenants that in an emergency he could always guess at what the landlords said.

"It was rather short," Mary admitted, "compared with the report in the *Argus*. Papa thought—" She stopped hastily.

"He thought it should have been longer?" asked Rob. Then before he had time to think of it, he had told her of his first meeting with the colonel.

"I remember papa was angry at the time," Mary said, "but you need not have been afraid of his recognizing you last night. He did recognize you."

"Did he?"

"Yes; but you were his guest."

Rob could not think of anything more to say, and he saw that Mary was about to bid him good morning. He found himself walking with her in the direction of the castle gates.

"This scenery reminds me of Scotland," he said.

"I love it," said Mary (man's only excellence over woman is that his awe of this word prevents his using it so lightly), "and I am glad that I shall be here until the season begins."

Rob had no idea what the season was, but he saw that some time Mary would be going away, and his face said, what would he do then?

"Then I go to London with the Merediths," she continued, adding thoughtfully, "I suppose you mean to go to London, Mr. Angus? My brother says that all literary men drift there."

"Yes, oh, yes," said Rob.

"Soon?"

"Immediately," he replied, recklessly.

They reached the gates, and, as Mary held out her hand, the small basket was tilted upon her arm, and a card fluttered out.

"It is a Christmas card a little boy in one of those houses gave me," she said, as Rob returned it to her. "Have you got many Christmas cards to-day, Mr. Angus?"

"None," said Rob.

"Not even from your relatives?" asked Mary, beginning to pity him more than was necessary.

"I have no relatives," he replied; "they are all dead."

"I was in Scotland two summers ago," Mary said, very softly, "at a place called Glen Quharity; papa was there shooting. But I don't suppose you know it?"

"Our Glen Quharity!" exclaimed Rob; "why, you must have passed through Thrums?"

"We were several times in Thrums. Have you been there?"

"I was born in it; I was never thirty miles away from it until I came here."

"Oh," cried Mary, "then you must be the literary—" She stopped and reddened.

"The literary saw-miller," said Rob, finishing her sentence; "that was what they called me, I know, at Glen Quharity Lodge."

Mary looked up at him with a new interest, for when she was there Glen Quharity had been full of the saw-miller, who could not only talk in Greek, but had a reputation for tossing the caber.

"Papa told me some months ago," she said, in surprise, "that the lite—, that you had joined the press in England, but he evidently did not know of your being in Silchester."

"But how could he have known anything about me?" asked Rob, surprised in turn.

"This is so strange," Mary answered. "Why, papa takes credit for having got you your appointment on the press."

"It was a minister, a Mr. Rorrison, who did that for me," said Rob; "indeed, he was so good that I could have joined the press a year ago by his help, had not circumstances compelled me to remain at home."

"I did not know the clergyman's name," Mary said, "but it was papa who spoke of you to him first. Don't you remember writing out this clergyman's sermon in shorthand, and a messenger's coming to you for your report on horseback next day?"

"Certainly I do," said Rob, "and he asked me to write it out in longhand as quickly as possible. That was how I got to know Mr. Rorrison; and, as I understood, he had sent for the report of the sermon, on hearing accidentally that I had taken it down, because he had some reason for wanting a copy of it."

"Perhaps that was how it was told to you after-

wards," Mary said, " but it was really papa who
wanted the sermon."

" I should like to know all about it," Rob said,
seeing that she hesitated. Colonel Abinger had not
seemed to him the kind of man who would send a
messenger on horseback about the country in quest
of sermons.

" I am afraid," Mary explained, " that it arose
out of a wager. This clergyman was staying at
the Lodge, but papa was the only other person
there who would go as far as Thrums to hear him
preach. I was not there that year, so I don't know
why papa went, but when he returned he told the
others that the sermon had been excellent. There
is surely an English church in Thrums, for I am
sure papa would not think a sermon excellent that
was preached in a chapel ? "

" There is," said Rob ; " but in Thrums it is
called the chapel."

" Well, some badinage arose out of papa's eu-
logy, and it ended in a bet that he could not tell
the others what this fine sermon was about. He
was to get a night to think it over. Papa took the
bet a little rashly, for when he put it to himself he
found that he could not even remember the text.
As he told me afterwards (here Mary smiled a
little), he had a general idea of the sermon, but
could not quite put it into words, and he was fearing that he would lose the wager (and be laughed

at, which always vexes papa), when he heard of your report. So a messenger was sent to Thrums for it — and papa won his bet."

"But how did Mr. Rorrison hear of my report, then?"

"Oh, I forgot; papa told him afterwards, and was so pleased with his victory, that when he heard Mr. Rorrison had influence with some press people, he suggested to him that something might be done for you."

"This is strange," said Rob, "and perhaps the strangest thing about it is that if Colonel Abinger could identify me with the saw-miller he would be sorry that he had interfered."

Mary saw the force of this so clearly that she could not contradict him.

"Surely," she said, "I heard when I was at the Lodge of your having a niece, and that you and the little child lived alone in the saw-mill?"

"Yes," Rob answered, hoarsely, "but she is dead. She wandered from home, and was found dead on a mountain-side."

"Was it long ago?" asked Mary, very softly.

"Only a few months ago," Rob said, making his answer as short as possible, for the death of Davy moved him still. "She was only four years old."

Mary's hand went half-way toward his involuntarily. His mouth was twitching. He knew how good she was.

" That card," he began, and hesitated.

" Oh, would you care to have it ? " said Mary.

But just then Colonel Abinger walked into them, somewhat amazed to see his daughter talking to one of the lower orders. Neither Rob nor Mary had any inclination to tell him that this was the Scotsman he had befriended.

" This is Mr. Angus, papa," said Mary, " who— who was with us last night."

" Mr. Angus and I have met before, I think," replied her father, recalling the fishing episode. His brow darkened, and Rob was ready for anything, but Colonel Abinger was a gentleman.

" I always wanted to see you again, Mr. Angus," he said, with an effort, " to ask you — what flies you were using that day ? "

Rob muttered something in answer, which the colonel did not try to catch. Mary smiled and bowed, and the next moment she had disappeared with her father down the avenue.

What followed cannot be explained. When Rob roused himself from his amazement at Mary Abinger's having been in Thrums without his feeling her presence, something made him go a few yards inside the castle grounds, and, lying lightly on the snow, he saw the Christmas card. He lifted it up as if it were a rare piece of china, and held it in his two hands as though it were a bird which might escape. He did not know whether it had dropped there of its own accord, and doubt and transport fought for victory on his face. At last he put the card exultingly into his pocket, his chest heaved, and he went toward Silchester whistling.

CHAPTER VII

THE GRAND PASSION?

ONE of the disappointments of life is that the persons we think we have reason to dislike are seldom altogether villains; they are not made sufficiently big for it. When we can go to sleep in an armchair this ceases to be a trouble, but it vexed Mary Abinger. Her villain of fiction, on being haughtily rejected, had at least left the heroine's home looking a little cowed. Sir Clement in the same circumstances had stayed on.

The colonel had looked forward resentfully for years to meeting this gentleman again, and giving him a piece of his stormy mind. When the opportunity came, however, Mary's father instead asked his unexpected visitor to remain for a week. Colonel Abinger thought he was thus magnanimous because his guest had been confidential with him, but it was perhaps rather because Sir Clement had explained how much he thought of him. To dislike our admirers is to be severe on ourselves, and is therefore not common.

The Dome had introduced the colonel to Sir Clement as well as to Rob. One day Colonel

118

THE GRAND PASSION?

Abinger had received by letter from a little hostelry in the neighbourhood the compliments of Sir Clement Dowton, and a request that he might be allowed to fish in the preserved water. All that Mary's father knew of Dowton at that time was that he had been lost to English society for half a dozen years. Once in many months the papers spoke of him as serving under Gordon in China, as being taken captive by an African king, as having settled down in a cattle ranche in the vicinity of Manitoba. His lawyers were probably aware of his whereabouts oftener than other persons. All that society knew was that he hated England because one of its daughters had married a curate. The colonel called at the inn, and found Sir Clement such an attentive listener that he thought the baronet's talk quite brilliant. A few days afterwards the stranger's traps were removed to the castle, and then he met Miss Abinger, who was recently home from school. He never spoke to her of his grudge against England.

It is only the unselfish men who think much, otherwise Colonel Abinger might have pondered a little over his guest. Dowton had spoken of himself as an enthusiastic angler, yet he let his flies drift down the stream like fallen leaves. He never remembered to go a-fishing until it was suggested to him. He had given his host several reasons for his long absence from his property, and told him he did not want the world to know that he was back in England, as he was not certain whether he would remain. The colonel at his request introduced him to the few visitors at the castle as Mr. Dowton, and was surprised to discover afterwards that they all knew his real name.

"I assure you," Mary's father said to him, "that they have not learned it from me. It is incomprehensible how a thing like that leaks out."

"I don't understand it," said Dowton, who, however, should have understood it, as he had taken the visitors aside and told them his real name himself. He seemed to do this not of his free will, but because he could not help it.

It never struck the colonel that his own society was not what tied Sir Clement to Dome Castle; for widowers with grown-up daughters are in a foreign land without interpreters. On that morning when the baronet vanished, nevertheless, the master of Dome Castle was the only person in it who did not think that it would soon lose its mistress, mere girl though she was.

Sir Clement's strange disappearance was accounted for at the castle, where alone it was properly known, in various ways. Miss Abinger, in the opinion of the servants' hall, held her head so high that there he was believed to have run away because she had said him no. Miss Abinger excused and blamed him alternately to herself until she found a dull satisfaction in looking upon him as the villain he might have been had his high forehead spoken true. As for the colonel, he ordered Mary (he had no need) never to mention the fellow's name to him, but mentioned it frequently himself.

Nothing had happened, so far as was known, to disturb the baronet's serenity; neither friends nor lawyers had been aware that he was in England, and he had received no letters. Mary remembered his occasional fits of despondency, but on the whole he seemed to revel in his visit, and had never looked happier than the night before he went. His traps were sent by the colonel in a fury to the little inn where he had at first taken up his abode, but it was not known at the castle whether he ever got them. Some months afterwards a letter from him appeared in the *Times*, dated from Suez, and from then until he reappeared at Dome Castle, the colonel, except when he spoke to himself, never heard the baronet's name mentioned.

Sir Clement must have been very impulsive, for on returning to the castle he had intended to treat Miss Abinger with courteous coldness, as if she had been responsible for his flight, and he had not seen her again for ten minutes before he asked her to marry him. He meant to explain his conduct in one way to the colonel, and he explained it in quite another way.

WHEN A MAN'S SINGLE

When Colonel Abinger took him into the smoking-room on Christmas Eve to hear what he had to say for himself, the baronet sank into a chair, with a look of contentment on his beautiful face that said he was glad to be there again. Then the colonel happened to mention Mary's name in such a way that he seemed to know of Sir Clement's proposal to her three years earlier. At once the baronet began another story from the one he had meant to tell, and though he soon discovered that he had credited his host with a knowledge the colonel did not possess, it was too late to draw back. So Mary's father heard to his amazement that the baronet had run away because he was in love with Miss Abinger. Colonel Abinger had read " The Scorn of Scorns," but it had taught him nothing.

" She was only a schoolgirl when you saw her last," he said, in bewilderment; " but I hardly see how that should have made you fly the house like — yes, like a thief."

Dowton looked sadly at him.

" I don't know," he said, speaking as if with reluctance, " that in any circumstances I should be justified in telling you the whole miserable story. Can you not guess it? When I came here I was not a free man."

" You were already married? "

" No, but I was engaged to be married."

"Did Mary know anything of this?"

"Nothing of that engagement, and but little, I think, of the attachment that grew up in my heart for her. I kept that to myself."

"She was too young," said the wise colonel, "to think of such things then; and even now I do not see why you should have left us as you did."

Sir Clement rose to his feet and paced the room in great agitation.

"It is hard," he said at last, "to speak of such a thing to another man. But let me tell you, Abinger, that when I was with you three years ago there were times when I thought I would lose my reason. Do you know what it is to have such a passion as that raging in your heart and yet have to stifle it? There were whole nights when I walked up and down my room till dawn. I trembled every time I saw Miss Abinger alone lest I should say that to her which I had no right to say. Her voice alone was sufficient to unman me. I felt that my only safety was in flight."

"I have run away from a woman myself in my time," the colonel said, with a grim chuckle. "There are occasions when it is the one thing to do, but this was surely not one of them, if Mary knew nothing."

"Sometimes I feared she did know that I cared for her. That is a hard thing to conceal, and, besides, I suppose I felt so wretched that I was not in a condition to act rationally. When I left the castle that day I had not the least intention of not returning."

" And since then you have been half round the world again ?   Are you married ? "

" No."

" Then I am to understand — "

" That she is dead," said Sir Clement, in a low voice.

There was a silence between them, which was at last broken by the colonel.

" What you have told me," he said, " is a great surprise, more especially with regard to my daughter.   Being but a child at the time, however, she could not, I am confident, have thought of you in any other light than as her father's friend.   It is, of course, on that footing that you return now ? "

" As her father's friend, certainly, I hope," said the baronet, firmly, " but I wish to tell you now that my regard for her has never changed.   I confess I would have been afraid to come back to you had not my longing to see her again given me courage."

" She has not the least idea of this," murmured the colonel, " not the least.   The fact is that Mary has lived so quietly with me here that she is still a child.   Miss Meredith, whom I daresay you have met here, has been almost her only friend, and I am quite certain that the thought of marriage has never crossed their minds. If you, or even if I, were to speak of such a thing to Mary it would only frighten her."

"I should not think of speaking to her on the subject at present," the baronet interposed, rather hurriedly, "but I thought it best to explain my position to you. You know what I am, that I have been almost a vagrant on the face of the earth since I reached manhood, but no one can see more clearly than I do myself how unworthy I am of her."

"I do not need to tell you," said the colonel, taking the baronet's hand, "that I used to like you, Dowton, and indeed I know no one whom I would prefer for a son-in-law. But you must be cautious with Mary."

"I shall be very cautious," said the baronet; indeed there is no hurry, none whatever."

Colonel Abinger would have brought the conversation to a close here, but there was something more for Dowton to say.

"I agree with you," he said, forgetting, perhaps, that the colonel had not spoken on this point, "that Miss Abinger should be kept ignorant for the present of the cause that drove me on that former occasion from the castle."

"It is the wisest course to adopt," said the colonel, looking as if he had thought the matter out step by step.

"The only thing I am doubtful about," continued Dowton, "is whether Miss Abinger will not think that she is entitled to some explanation. She cannot, I fear, have forgotten the circumstances of my departure."

"Make your mind easy on that score," said the colonel; "the best proof that Mary gave the matter little thought, even at the time, is that she did not speak of it to me. Sweet seventeen has always a short memory."

"But I have sometimes thought since that Miss Abinger did care for me a little, in which case she would have unfortunate cause to resent my flight."

While he spoke the baronet was looking anxiously into the colonel's face.

"I can give you my word for it," said the colonel, cheerily, "that she did not give your disappearance two thoughts; and now I much question whether she will recognize you."

Dowton's face clouded, but the other misinterpreted the shadow.

"So put your mind at rest," said the colonel, kindly, "and trust an old stager like myself for being able to read into a woman's heart."

Shortly afterwards Colonel Abinger left his guest, and for nearly five minutes the baronet looked dejected. It is sometimes advantageous to hear that a lady with whom you have watched the moon rise has forgotten your very name, but it is never complimentary. By and by, however, Sir

Clement's sense of humour drove the gloom from his chiselled face, and a glass bracket over the mantelpiece told him that he was laughing heartily.

It was a small breakfast party at the castle next morning, Sir Clement and Greybrooke being the only guests, but the baronet was so gay and morose by turns that he might have been two persons. In the middle of a laugh at some remark of the captain's, he would break off with a sigh, and immediately after sadly declining another cup of coffee from Mary, he said something humorous to her father. The one mood was natural to him and the other forced, but it would have been difficult to decide which was which. It is, however, one of the hardest things in life to remain miserable for any length of time on a stretch. When Dowton found himself alone with Mary his fingers were playing an exhilarating tune on the window-sill, but as he looked at her his hands fell to his side, and there was pathos in his fine eyes. Drawn toward her, he took a step forward, but Miss Abinger said " No " so decisively that he stopped irresolute.

" I shall be leaving the castle in an hour," Sir Clement said, slowly.

" Papa told me," said Mary, " that he had prevailed upon you to remain for a week."

" He pressed me to do so, and I consented, but you have changed everything since then. Ah, Mary — "

" Miss Abinger," said Mary.

" Miss Abinger, if you would only listen to
what I have to say. I can explain everything,
I —"

" There is nothing to explain," said Mary, " nothing that I have either a right or a desire to hear.
Please not to return to this subject again. I said
everything there was to say last night."

The baronet's face paled, and he bowed his head
in deep dejection. His voice was trembling a
little, and he observed it with gratification as he
answered —

" Then, I suppose, I must bid you good-bye ? "

" Good-bye," said Mary. " Does papa know
you are going ? "

" I promised him to stay on," said Sir Clement,
" and I can hardly expect him to forgive me if I
change my mind."

This was put almost in the form of a question,
and Mary thought she understood it.

" Then you mean to remain ? " she asked.

" You compel me to go," he replied, dolefully.

" Oh no," said Mary, " I have nothing to do
with your going or staying."

" But it — it would hardly do for me to remain after what took place last night," said the
baronet, in the tone of one who was open to con-
tradiction.

For the first time in the conversation Mary

smiled. It was not, however, the smile every man would care to see at his own expense.

"If you were to go now," she said, "you would not be fulfilling your promise to papa, and I know that men do not like to break their word to — to other men."

"Then you think I ought to stay?" asked Sir Clement, eagerly.

"It is for you to think," said Mary.

"Perhaps, then, I ought to remain — for Colonel Abinger's sake," said the baronet.

Mary did not answer.

"Only for a few days," he continued, almost appealingly.

"Very well," said Mary.

"And you won't think the worse of me for it?" asked Dowton, anxiously. "Of course, if I were to consult my own wishes I would go now. but as I promised Colonel Abinger — "

"You will remain out of consideration for papa. How could I think worse of you for that?"

Mary rose to leave the room, and as Sir Clement opened the door for her he said —

"We shall say nothing of all this to Colonel Abinger?"

"Oh no, certainly not," said Mary.

She glanced up in his face, her mouth twisted slightly to one side, as it had a habit of doing when she felt disdainful, and the glory of her beauty filled him of a sudden. The baronet pushed the door close and turned to her passionately, a film over his eyes, and his hands outstretched.

"Mary," he cried, "is there no hope for me?"

"No," said Mary, opening the door for herself, and passing out.

"Sir Clement stood there motionless for a minute. Then he crossed to the fireplace, and sank into a luxuriously cushioned chair. The sunlight came back to his noble face.

"This is grand, glorious," he murmured, in an ecstasy of enjoyment.

In the days that followed, the baronet's behaviour was a little peculiar. Occasionally at meals he seemed to remember that a rejected lover ought not to have a good appetite. If, when he was smoking in the grounds, he saw Mary approaching, he covertly dropped his cigar. When he knew that she was sitting at a window he would pace up and down the walk with his head bent as if life had lost its interest to him. By and by his mind wandered, on these occasions, to more cheerful matters, and he would start to find that he had been smiling to himself and swishing his cane playfully, like a man who walked on air. It might have been said of him that he tried to be miserable and found it hard work.

Will, who discovered that the baronet did not know what l. b. w. meant, could not, nevertheless, despise a man who had shot lions, but he never had quite the same respect for the king of beasts again. As for Greybrooke, he rather liked Sir Clement, because he knew that Nell (in her own words) " loathed, hated, and despised " him.

Greybrooke had two severe disappointments that holiday, both of which were to be traced to the capricious Nell. It had dawned on him that she could not help liking him a little if she saw him take a famous jump over the Dome, known to legend as the " Robber's Leap." The robber had lost his life in trying to leap the stream, but the captain practised in the castle grounds until he felt that he could clear it. Then he formally invited Miss Meredith to come and see him do it, and she told him instead that he was wicked. The captain and Will went back silently to the castle, wondering what on earth she would like.

Greybrooke's other disappointment was still more grievous. One evening he and Will returned to the castle late for dinner, an offence the colonel found it hard to overlook, although they were going back to school on the following day. Will reached the dining-room first, and his father frowned on him.

" You are a quarter of an hour late, William," said the colonel, sternly. " Where have you been ? "

Will hesitated.

"Do you remember," he said, at last, "a man called Angus, who was here reporting on Christmas Eve?"

Mary laid down her knife and fork.

"A painfully powerful-looking man," said Dowton, "in hob-nailed boots. I remember him."

"Well, we have been calling on him," said Will.

"Calling on him, calling on that impudent newspaper man!" exclaimed the colonel; "what do you mean?"

"Greybrooke had a row with him some time ago," said Will; "I don't know what about, because it was private; but the captain has been looking for the fellow for a fortnight to lick him —I mean punish him. We came upon him two days ago, near the castle gates."

Here Will paused, as if he would prefer to jump what followed.

"And did your friend 'lick' him then?" asked the colonel, at which Will shook his head.

"Why not?" asked Sir Clement.

"Well," said Will, reluctantly, "the fellow wouldn't let him. He—he lifted Greybrooke up in his arms, and — and dropped him over the hedge."

Mary could not help laughing.

"The beggar — I mean the fellow — must have muscles like ivy roots," Will blurted out, admiringly.

"I fancy," said Dowton, "that I have seen him near the gates several times during the last week."

"Very likely," said the colonel, shortly. "I caught him poaching in the Dome some months ago. There is something bad about that man."

"Papa!" said Mary.

At this moment Greybrooke entered.

"So, Mr. Greybrooke," said the colonel, "I hear you nave been in Silchester avenging an insult."

The captain looked at Will, who nodded.

"I went there, admitted Greybrooke, blushing, "to horsewhip a reporter fellow, but he had run away."

"Run away?"

"Yes. Did not Will tell you? We called at the *Mirror* office, and were told that Angus had bolted to London two days ago."

"And the worst of it," interposed Will, "is that he ran off without paying his landlady's bill."

"I knew that man was a rascal," exclaimed the colonel.

Mary flushed.

"I don't believe it," she said

"You don't believe it," repeated her father, angrily; "and why not, pray?"

"Because — because I don't," said Mary.

CHAPTER VIII

MARY was wrong. It was quite true that Rob had
run away to London without paying his landlady's
bill.

The immediate result of his meeting with Miss
Abinger had been to make him undertake double
work, and not do it. Looking in at shop-windows,
where he saw hats that he thought would just suit
Mary (he had a good deal to learn yet), it came
upon him that he was wasting his time. Then he
hurried home, contemptuous of all the rest of Silchester, to write an article for a London paper,
and when he next came to himself, half an hour
afterwards, he was sitting before a blank sheet of
copy paper. He began to review a book, and
found himself gazing at a Christmas card. He
tried to think out the action of a government, and
thought out a ring on Miss Abinger's finger instead. Three nights running he dreamt that he
was married, and woke up quaking.

Without much misgiving Rob heard it said in
Silchester that there was some one staying at Dome

Castle who was to be its mistress's husband. On discovering that they referred to Dowton, and not being versed in the wonderful ways of woman, he told himself that this was impossible. A cynic would have pointed out that Mary had now had several days in which to change her mind. Cynics are persons who make themselves the measure of other people.

The philosopher who remarked that the obvious truths are those which are most often missed, was probably referring to the time it takes a man to discover that he is in love. Women are quicker because they are on the outlook. It took Rob two days, and when it came upon him checked his breathing. After that he bore it like a man. Another discovery he had to make was that, after all, he was nobody in particular. This took him longer.

Although the manner of his going to London was unexpected, Rob had thought out solidly the inducements to go. Ten minutes or so after he knew that he wanted to marry Mary Abinger, he made up his mind to try to do it. The only obstacles he saw in his way were, that she was not in love with him, and lack of income. Feeling that he was an uncommon type of man (if people would only see it) he resolved to remove this second difficulty first. The saw-mill and the castle side by side did not rise up and frighten him, and for the time he succeeded in not thinking about Colonel Abinger. Nothing is hopeless if we want it very much.

Rob calculated that if he remained on the *Mirror* for another dozen years or so, and Mr. Licquorish continued to think that it would not be cheaper to do without him, he might reach a salary of £200 per annum. As that was not sufficient, he made up his mind to leave Silchester.

There was only one place to go to. Rob thought of London until he felt that it was the guardian from whom he would have to ask Mary Abinger; he pictured her there during the season, until London, which he had never seen, began to assume a homely aspect. It was the place in which he was to win or lose his battle. To whom is London much more? It is the clergyman's name for his church, the lawyer's for his office, the politician's for St. Stephen's, the cabman's for his stand.

There was not a man on the press in Silchester who did not hunger for Fleet Street, but they were all afraid to beard it. They knew it as a rabbit-warren; as the closest street in a city where the bootblack has his sycophants, and you have to battle for exclusive right to sweep a crossing. The fight forward had been grimmer to Rob, however, than to his fellows, and he had never been quite beaten. He was alone in the world, and poverty was like an old friend. There was only one journalist in London whom he knew even by name, and he wrote to him for advice. This was Mr. John Rorrison, a son of the minister whose assistance had brought Rob to Silchester. Rorrison was understood to be practically editing a great London newspaper, which is what is understood of a great many journalists until you make inquiries, but he wrote back to Rob asking him why he wanted to die before his time. You collectors who want an editor's autograph may rely upon having it by return of post if you write threatening to come to London with the hope that he will do something for you. Rorrison's answer discomfited Rob for five minutes, and then, going out, he caught a glimpse of Mary Abinger in the Merediths' carriage. He tore up the letter, and saw that London was worth risking.

One forenoon Rob set out for the office to tell Mr. Licquorish of his determination. He knew that the entire staff would think him demented, but he could not see that he was acting rashly. He had worked it all out in his mind, and even tranquilly faced possible starvation. Rob was congratulating himself on not having given way to impulse when he reached the railway station.

His way from his lodgings to the office led past the station, and as he had done scores of times before, he went inside   To Rob all the romance of

Silchester was concentrated there; nothing stirred
him so much as a panting engine; the shunting
of carriages, the bustle of passengers, the porters
rattling to and fro with luggage, the trains twisting
serpent-like into the station and stealing out in a
glory to be gone, sent the blood to his head. On
Saturday nights, when he was free, any one calling
at the station would have been sure to find him on
the platform from which the train starts for London.
His heart had sunk every time it went off without
him.

Rob woke up from a dream of Fleet Street to
see the porters slamming the doors of the London
train. He saw the guard's hand upraised, and
heard the carriages rattle as the restive engine took
them unawares. Then came the warning whistle,
and the train moved off. For a second of time
Rob felt that he had lost London, and he started
forward. Some one near him shouted, and then
he came upon the train all at once, a door opened,
and he shot in. When he came to himself, Silchester was a cloud climbing to the sky behind
him, and he was on his way to London.

Rob's first feeling was that the other people in
the carriage must know what he had done. He
was relieved to find that his companions were only
an old gentleman who spoke fiercely to his newspaper because it was reluctant to turn inside out,
a little girl who had got in at Silchester and con-

sumed thirteen halfpenny buns before she was five
miles distant from it, and a young woman, evidently
a nurse, with a baby in her arms. The baby was
noisy for a time, but Rob gave it a look that kept
it silent for the rest of the journey. He told himself that he would get out at the first station, but
when the train stopped at it he sat on. He twisted
himself into a corner to count his money covertly,
and found that it came to four pounds odd. He
also took the Christmas card from his pocket, but
replaced it hastily, feeling that the old gentleman
and the little girl were looking at him. A feeling
of elation grew upon him as he saw that whatever
might happen afterwards he must be in London
shortly, and his mind ran on the letters he would
write to Mr. Licquorish and his landlady. In lieu
of his ticket he handed over twelve shillings to the
guard, under whose eyes he did not feel comfortable, and he calculated that he owed his landlady
over two pounds. He would send it to her and ask
her to forward his things to London. Mr. Licquorish, however, might threaten him with the law
if he did not return. But then the *Mirror* owed
Rob several pounds at that moment, and if he did
not claim it in person it would remain in Mr.
Licquorish's pockets. There was no saying how
far that consideration would affect the editor. Rob
saw a charge of dishonesty rise up and confront
him, and he drew back from it. A moment after-

wards he looked it in the face, and it receded. He took his pipe from his pocket.

"This is not a smoking carriage," gasped the little girl, so promptly that it almost seemed as if she had been waiting her opportunity ever since the train started. Rob looked at her. She seemed about eight, but her eye was merciless. He thrust his pipe back into its case, feeling cowed at last.

The nurse who had been looking at Rob and blushing when she caught his eye, got out with her charge at a side station, and he helped her rather awkwardly to alight "Don't mention it," he said, in answer to her thanks.

"Not a word; I'm not that kind," she replied, so eagerly that he started back in alarm, to find the little girl looking suspiciously at him.

As Rob stepped out of the train at King's Cross he realized sharply that he was alone in the world. He did not know where to go now, and his heart sank for a time as he paced the platform irresolutely, feeling that it was his last link to Silchester. He turned into the booking-office to consult a time-table, and noticed against the wall a railway map of London. For a long time he stood looking at it, and as he traced the river, the streets familiar to him by name, the districts and buildings which were household words to him, he felt that he must live in London somehow. He discovered Fleet Street in the map, and studied the best way of getting to it from King's Cross. Then grasping his stick firmly, he took possession of London as calmly as he could.

Rob never found any difficulty afterwards in picking out the shabby eating-house in which he had his first meal in London. Gray's Inn Road remained to him always its most romantic street because he went down it first. He walked into the roar of London in Holborn, and never forgot the alley into which he retreated to discover if he had suddenly become deaf. He wondered when the crowd would pass. Years afterwards he turned into Fetter Lane, and suddenly there came back to his mind the thoughts that had held him as he went down it the day he arrived in London.

A certain awe came upon Rob as he went down Fleet Street on the one side, and up it on the other. He could not resist looking into the faces of the persons who passed him, and wondering if they edited the *Times*. The lean man who was in such a hurry that wherever he had to go he would soon be there, might be a man of letters whom Rob knew by heart, but perhaps he was only a broken journalist with his eye on half a crown. The mild-looking man whom Rob smiled at because, when he was half way across the street, he lost his head and was chased out of sight by half a dozen hansom cabs, was a war correspondent who had been so long in Africa that the perils of a London crossing unmanned him. The youth who was on his way home with a pork chop in his pocket edited a society journal. Rob did not recognize a distinguished poet in a little stout man who was looking pensively at a barrowful of walnuts, and he was mistaken in thinking that the bearded gentleman who held his head so high must be somebody in particular. Rob observed a pale young man gazing wistfully at him, and wondered if he was a thief or a sub-editor. He was merely an aspirant who had come to London that morning to make his fortune, and he took Rob for a leader writer at the least. The offices, however, and even the public buildings, the shops, the narrowness of the streets, all disappointed Rob. The houses seemed squeezed together for economy of space, like a closed concertina. Nothing quite fulfilled his expectations but the big letter holes in the district postal offices. He had not been sufficiently long in London to feel its greatest charm, which has been expressed in many ways by poet, wit, business man and philosopher, but comes to this, that it is the only city in the world in whose streets you can eat penny buns without people's turning round to look at you.

In a few days Rob was part of London. His Silchester landlady had forwarded him his things, and Mr. Licquorish had washed his hands of him. The editor of the *Mirror's* letter amounted to a lament that a man whom he had allowed to do two men's work for half a man's wages should have treated him thus. Mr. Licquorish, however, had conceived the idea of "forcing" John Milton, and so saving a reporter, and he did not insist on Rob's returning. He expressed a hope that his ex-reporter would do well in London, and a fear, amounting to a conviction, that he would not. But he sent the three pounds due to him in wages, pointing out, justifiably enough, that, strictly speaking, Rob owed him a month's salary. Rob had not expected such liberality, and from that time always admitted that there must have been a heroic vein in Mr. Licquorish after all.

Rob established himself in a little back room in Islington, so small that a fairly truthful journalist might have said of it, in an article, that you had to climb the table to reach the fireplace, and to lift out the easy-chair before you could get out at the door. The room was over a grocer's shop, whose window bore the announcement: "Eggs, new laid, 1s. 3d.; eggs, fresh, 1s. 2d.; eggs, warranted, 1s.; eggs, 10d." A shop across the way hinted at the reputation of the neighbourhood in the polite placard, "Trust in the Lord: every other person cash."

The only ornament Rob added to the room was the Christmas card in a frame. He placed this on his mantelpiece and looked at it frequently, but

143

when he heard his landlady coming he slipped it
back into his pocket. Yet he would have liked
at times to have the courage to leave it there.
Though he wanted to be a literary man he began
his career in London with a little sense, for he
wrote articles to editors instead of calling at the
offices, and he had the good fortune to have no in-
troductions. The only pressman who ever made
anything by insisting on seeing the editor, was one
— a Scotsman, no doubt — who got him alone and
threatened to break his head if he did not find an
opening for him. The editor saw that this was the
sort of man who had made up his mind to get on,
and yielded.

During his first month in London, Rob wrote
thirty articles, and took them to the different offices in order to save the postage. There were
many other men in the streets at night doing the
same thing. He got fifteen articles back by return
of post, and never saw the others again. But here
was the stuff Rob was made of. The thirty having been rejected, he dined on bread-and-cheese,
and began the thirty-first. It was accepted by the
Minotaur, a weekly paper. Rob drew a sigh of
exultation as he got his first proof in London, and
remembered that he had written the article in two
hours. The payment, he understood, would be
two pounds at least, and at the rate of two articles
a day, working six days a week, this would mean

over six hundred a year. Rob had another look at the Christmas card, and thought it smiled. Every man is a fool now and then.

Except to his landlady, who thought that he dined out, Rob had not spoken to a soul since he arrived in London. To celebrate his first proof he resolved to call on Rorrison. He had not done so earlier because he thought that Rorrison would not be glad to see him. Though he had kept his disappointments to himself, however, he felt that he must remark casually to some one that he was writing for the *Minotaur*.

Rorrison had chambers at the top of one of the Inns of Court, and as he had sported his oak, Rob ought not to have knocked. He knew no better, however, and Rorrison came grumbling to the door. He was a full-bodied man of middle-age, with a noticeably heavy chin, and wore a long dressing-gown.

" I'm Angus from Silchester," Rob explained.

Rorrison's countenance fell. His occupation largely consisted in avoiding literary young men, who, he knew, were thirsting to take him aside and ask him to get them sub-editorships.

" I'm glad to see you," he said, gloomily; " come in."

What Rob first noticed in the sitting-room was that it was all in shadow, except one corner, whose many colours dazzled the eye. Suspended over this part of the room on a gas bracket was a great Japanese umbrella without a handle. This formed an awning for a large cane-chair and a tobacco-table, which also held a lamp, and Rorrison had been lolling on the chair looking at a Gladstone bag on the hearthrug until he felt that he was busy packing.

"Mind the umbrella," he said to his visitor.

The next moment a little black hole that had been widening in the Japanese paper just above the lamp cracked and broke, and a tongue of flame swept up the umbrella. Rob sprang forward in horror, but Rorrison only sighed.

"That makes the third this week," he said, "but let it blaze. I used to think they would set the place on fire, but somehow they don't do it. Don't give the thing the satisfaction of seeming to notice it."

The umbrella had been frizzled in a second, and its particles were already trembling through the room like flakes of snow.

"You have just been in time to find me," Rorrison said; "I start to-morrow afternoon for Egypt in the special correspondent business."

"I envy you," said Rob, and then told the manner of his coming to London.

"It was a mad thing to do," said Rorrison, looking at him, not without approval, "but the best journalists frequently begin in that way. I suppose you have been besieging the newspaper offices since you arrived; any result?"

"I had a proof from the *Minotaur* this evening," said Rob.

Rorrison blew some rings of smoke into the air and ran his finger through them. Then he turned proudly to Rob, and saw that Rob was looking proudly at him.

"Ah, what did you say?" asked Rorrison.

"The *Minotaur* has accepted one of my things," said Rob.

Rorrison said "Hum," and then hesitated.

"It is best that you should know the truth," he said at last. "No doubt you expect to be paid by the *Minotaur*, but I am afraid there is little hope of that — unless you dun them. A friend of mine sent them something lately, and Roper (the editor, you know) wrote asking him for more. He sent two or three other things, and then called at the office, expecting to be paid."

"Was he not?"

"On the contrary," said Rorrison, "Roper asked him for the loan of five pounds."

Rob's face grew so long that even the hardened Rorrison tried to feel for him.

"You need not let an experience that every one has to pass through dishearten you," he said. "There are only about a dozen papers in London that are worth writing for, but I can give you a good account of them. Not only do they pay handsomely, but the majority are open to contributions from any one. Don't you believe what one reads about newspaper rings. Everything sent in is looked at, and if it is suitable any editor is glad to have it. Men fail to get a footing on the press because — well, as a rule, because they are stupid."

" I am glad to hear you say that," said Rob, " and yet I had thirty articles rejected before the *Minotaur* accepted that one."

" Yes, and you will have another thirty rejected if they are of the same kind. You beginners seem able to write nothing but your views on politics, and your reflections on art, and your theories of life, which you sometimes even think original. Editors won't have that, because their readers don't want it. Every paper has its regular staff of leader-writers, and what is wanted from the outside is freshness. An editor tosses aside your column and a half about evolution, but is glad to have a paragraph saying that you saw Herbert Spencer the day before yesterday gazing solemnly for ten minutes in at a milliner's window. Fleet Street at this moment is simply running with men who want to air their views about things in general."

" I suppose so," said Rob, dolefully.

" Yes, and each thinks himself as original as he is profound, though they have only to meet to discover that they repeat each other. The pity of it is, that all of them could get on to some extent if they would send in what is wanted. There is copy in every man you meet, and, as a journalist on this stair says, when you do meet him you feel inclined to tear it out of him and use it yourself."

"What sort of copy?" asked Rob.

"They should write of the things they have seen. Newspaper readers have an insatiable appetite for knowing how that part of the world lives with which they are not familiar. They want to know how the Norwegians cook their dinners and build their houses and ask each other in marriage."

"But I have never been out of Britain."

"Neither was Shakespeare. There are thousands of articles in Scotland yet. You must know a good deal about the Scottish weavers — well, there are articles in them. Describe the daily life of a gillie: 'The Gillie at Home' is a promising title. Were you ever snowed-up in your saw-mill? Whether you were or not, there is a seasonable subject for January. 'Yule in a Scottish Village' also sounds well, and there is a safe article in a Highland gathering."

"These must have been done before, though," said Rob.

"Of course they have," answered Rorrison; "but do them in your own way: the public has no memory, and besides, new publics are always springing up."

"I am glad I came to see you," said Rob, brightening considerably; "I never thought of these things."

"Of course you need not confine yourself to them. Write on politics if you will, but don't merely say what you yourself think; rather tell, for instance, what is the political situation in the country parts known to you. That should be more interesting and valuable than your individual views. But I may tell you that, if you have the journalistic faculty, you will always be on the look-out for possible articles. The man on this stair I have mentioned to you would have had an article out of you before he had talked with you as long as I have done. You must have heard of Noble Simms?"

"Yes, I know his novel," said Rob; "I should like immensely to meet him."

"I must leave you an introduction to him," said Rorrison; "he wakens most people up, though you would scarcely think it to look at him. You see this pipe here? Simms saw me mending it with sealing-wax one day, and two days afterwards there was an article about it in the *Scalping Knife*. When I went off for my holidays last summer I asked him to look in here occasionally and turn a new cheese which had been sent me from the country. Of course he forgot to do it, but I denounced him on my return for not keeping his

solemn promise, so he revenged himself by publishing an article entitled 'Rorrison's Oil-Painting.'
In this it was explained that just before Rorrison
went off for a holiday he got a present of an oil-
painting. Remembering when he had got to Paris
that the painting, which had come to him wet from
the easel, had been left lying on his table, he telegraphed to the writer to have it put away out of
reach of dust and the cat. The writer promised to
do so, but when Rorrison returned he found the
picture lying just where he left it. He rushed off
to his friend's room to upbraid him, and did it so
effectually that the friend says in his article, 'I
will never do a good turn for Rorrison again!'"

"But why," asked Rob, " did he turn the cheese
into an oil-painting?"

"Ah, there you have the journalistic instinct
again. You see a cheese is too plebeian a thing to
form the subject of an article in the *Scalping Knife*,
so Simms made a painting of it. He has had my
Chinese umbrella from several points of view in
three different papers. When I play on his piano
I put scraps of paper on the notes to guide me,
and he made his three guineas out of that. Once
I challenged him to write an article on a straw
that was sticking to the sill of my window, and it
was one of the most interesting things he ever did.

Then there was the box of old clothes and other
odds and ends that he promised to store for me

when I changed my rooms. He sold the lot to a hawker for a pair of flower-pots, and wrote an article on the transaction. Subsequently he had another article on the flower-pots; and when I appeared to claim my belongings he got a third article out of that."

" I suppose he reads a great deal ? " said Rob.

" He seldom opens a book," answered Rorrison; " indeed, when he requires to consult a work of reference he goes to the Strand and does his reading at a bookstall. I don't think he was ever in the British Museum."

Rob laughed.

" At the same time," he said, " I don't think Mr Noble Simms could get any copy out of me."

Just then some one shuffled into the passage, and the door opened.

CHAPTER IX

THE new-comer was a young man with an impassive face and weary eyes, who, as he slouched in, described a parabola in the air with one of his feet, which was his way of keeping a burned slipper on. Rorrison introduced him to Rob as Mr. Noble Simms, after which Simms took himself into a corner of the room, like a man who has paid for his seat in a railway compartment and refuses to be drawn into conversation. He would have been a handsome man had he had a little more interest in himself.

"I thought you told me you were going out tonight," said Rorrison.

"I meant to go," Simms answered, "but when I rang for my boots the housekeeper thought I asked for water, and brought it, so, rather than explain matters to her, I drank the water and remained indoors."

"I read your book lately, Mr. Simms," Rob said, after he had helped himself to tobacco from Simms's pouch, "Try my tobacco," being the press form of salutation.

"You did not buy the second volume, did you?" asked Simms, with a show of interest, and Rob had to admit that he got the novel from a library.

"Excuse my asking you," Simms continued, in his painfully low voice; "I had a special reason. You see I happen to know that, besides what went to the libraries, there were in all six copies of my book sold. My admirer bought two, and I myself bought three and two-thirds, so that only one volume remains to be accounted for. I like to think that the purchaser was a lady."

"But how did it come about," inquired Rob, while Rorrison smoked on imperturbably, "that the volumes were on sale singly?"

"That was to tempt a public," said Simms, gravely, "who would not take kindly to the three volumes together. It is a long story, though."

Here he paused, as if anxious to escape out of the conversation.

"No blarney, Simms," expostulated Rorrison. "I forgot to tell you, Angus, that this man always means (when he happens to have a meaning) the reverse of what he says."

"Don't mind Rorrison," said Simms to Rob. "It was in this way. My great work of fiction did fairly well at the libraries, owing to a mistake Mudie made about the name. He ordered a number of copies under the impression that the book was by the popular novelist, Simmons, and when the mistake was found out he was too honourable to draw back. The surplus copies, however, would not sell at all. My publisher offered them as Saturday evening presents to his young men, but they always left them on their desks; so next he tried the second-hand book-shops, in the hope that people from the country would buy the three volumes because they looked so cheap at two shillings. However, even the label ' Published at 31s. 6d. : offered for 2s.,' was barren of results. I used to stand in an alley near one of these book-shops, and watch the people handling my novel."

" But no one made an offer for it ? "

" Not at two shillings, but when it came down to one-and-sixpence an elderly man with spectacles very nearly bought it. He was undecided between it and a Trigonometry, but in the end he went off with the Trigonometry. Then a young lady in grey and pink seemed interested in it. I watched her reading the bit about Lord John entering the drawing-room suddenly and finding Henry on his knees, and once I distinctly saw her smile."

" She might have bought the novel if only to see how it ended."

" Ah, I have always been of opinion that she would have done so, had she not most unfortunately, in her eagerness to learn what Henry said when he and Eleanor went into the conservatory, knocked a row of books over with her elbow. That frightened her, and she took to flight."

" Most unfortunate," said Rob, solemnly, though he was already beginning to understand Simms — as Simms was on the surface.

" I had a still greater disappointment," continued the author, " a few days afterwards. By this time the book was marked ' Very Amusing, 1s., worth 1s. 6d. ; ' and when I saw a pale-looking young man, who had been examining it, enter the shop, I thought the novel was as good as sold. My excitement was intense when a shopman came out for the three volumes and carried them inside, but I was puzzled on seeing the young gentleman depart, apparently without having made a purchase. Consider my feelings when the shopman replaced the three volumes on his shelf with the new label, ' 924 pp., 8d. ; worth 1s.' "

" Surely it found a purchaser now ? "

" Alas, no. The only man who seemed to be attracted by it at eightpence turned out to be the author of ' John Mordaunt's Christmas Box ' (' Thrilling ! Published at 6s. ; offered at 1s. 3d.'), who was hanging about in the interests of his own work."

" Did it come down to ' Sixpence, worth ninepence ? ' "

" No ; when I returned to the spot next day I found volumes One and Three in the ' 2d. any vol.'

box, and I carried them away myself. What became of volume Two I have never been able to discover. I rummaged the box for it in vain."

"As a matter of fact, Angus," remarked Rorrison, "the novel is now in its third edition."

"I always understood that it had done well," said Rob.

"The fourth time I asked for it at Mudie's," said Simms, the latter half of whose sentences were sometimes scarcely audible, "I inquired how it was doing, and was told that it had been already asked for three times. Curiously enough there is a general impression that it has been a great success, and for that I have to thank one man."

"The admirer of whom you spoke?"

"Yes, my admirer, as I love to call him. I first heard of him as a business gentleman living at Shepherd's Bush, who spoke with rapture of my novel to any chance acquaintances he made on the tops of 'buses. Then my aunt told me that a young lady knew a stout man living at Shepherd's Bush who could talk of nothing but my book; and on inquiry at my publisher's I learnt that a gentleman answering to this description had bought two copies. I heard of my admirer from different quarters for the next month, until a great longing rose in me to see him, to clasp his hand, to ask what part of the book he liked best, at the least to walk up and down past his windows, feeling that two men who appreciated each other were only separated by a pane of glass."

"Did you ever discover who he was?"

"I did. He lives at 42, Lavender Crescent, Shepherd's Bush, and his name is Henry Gilding."

"Well?" said Rob, seeing Simms pause, as if this was all.

"I am afraid, Mr. Angus," the author murmured in reply, "that you did not read the powerful and harrowing tale very carefully, or you would remember that my hero's name was also Henry Gilding."

"Well, but what of that?"

"There is everything in that. It is what made the Shepherd's Bush gentleman my admirer for life. He considers it the strangest and most diverting thing in his experience, and every night, I believe, after dinner, his eldest daughter has to read out to him the passages in which the Henry Gildings are thickest. He chuckles over the extraordinary coincidence still. He could take that joke with him to the seaside for a month, and it would keep him in humour all the time."

"Have done, Simms, have done," said Rorrison; "Angus is one of us, or wants to be, at all events. The *Minotaur* is printing one of his things, and I have been giving him some sage advice."

"Any man," said Simms, "will do well on the Press if he is stupid enough; even Rorrison has done well."

"I have just been telling him," responded Ror-rison, "that the stupid men fail."

"I don't consider you a failure, Rorrison," said Simms, in mild surprise. "What stock-in-trade a literary hand requires, Mr. Angus, is a fire to dry his writing at, jam or honey with which to gum old stamps on to envelopes, and an antimacassar."

"An antimacassar?" Rob repeated.

"Yes; you pluck the thread with which to sew your copy together out of the antimacassar. When my antimacassars are at the wash I have to take a holiday."

"Well, well, Simms," said Rorrison, "I like you best when you are taciturn."

"So do I," said Simms.

"You might give Angus some advice about the likeliest papers for which to write. London is new to him."

"The fact is, Mr. Angus," said Simms, more seriously, "that advice in such a matter is merely talk thrown away. If you have the journalistic instinct, which includes a determination not to be beaten as well as an aptitude for selecting the proper subjects, you will by and by find an editor who believes in you. Many men of genuine liter-ary ability have failed on the Press because they did not have that instinct, and they have attacked journalism in their books in consequence."

"I am not sure that I know what the journalistic

instinct precisely is," Rob said, "and still less whether I possess it."

" Ah, just let me put you through your paces," replied Simms. "Suppose yourself up for an exam. in journalism, and that I am your examiner. Question One : ' The house was soon on fire ; much sympathy is expressed with the suffererers.' Can you translate that into newspaper English ? "

" Let me see," answered Rob, entering into the spirit of the examination. " How would this do : ' In a moment the edifice was enveloped in shooting tongues of flame ; the appalling catastrophe has plunged the whole street into the gloom of night ' ? "

"Good. Question Two : A man hangs himself ; what is the technical heading for this ? "

" Either ' Shocking Occurrence ' or ' Rash Act.' "

" Question Three : ' *Pabulum*,' ' *Cela va sans dire*,' ' *Par excellence*,' ' *Ne plus ultra*.' What are these ? Are there any more of them ? "

" They are scholarship," replied Rob, " and there are two more, namely, ' *tour de force* ' and ' *terra firma*.' "

" Question Four : ' A. (a soldier) dies at 6 p.m. with his back to the foe. B. (a philanthropist) dies at 1 a.m. : which of these, speaking technically, would you call a creditable death ? "

" The soldier's, because time was given to set it."

" Quite right. Question Five : Have you ever

known a newspaper which did not have the largest
circulation in its district, and was not the most in-
fluential advertising medium ? "

" Never."

" Question Six : Mr. Gladstone rises to speak in
the House of Commons at 2 a.m. What would be
the sub-editor's probable remark on receiving the
opening words of the speech, and how would he
break the news to the editor ? How would the
editor be likely to take it ? "

" I prefer," said Rob, " not to answer that question."

" Well, Mr. Angus," said Simms, tiring of the
examination, " you have passed with honours."

The conversation turned to Rorrison's coming
work in Egypt, and by and by Simms rose to go.

" Your stick, I suppose, Mr. Angus ? " he said,
taking Rob's thick staff from a corner.

" Yes," answered Rob, " it has only a heavy
knob, you see, for a handle, and a doctor once told
me that if I continued to press so heavily on it I
might suffer from some disease in the palm of the
hand."

" I never heard of that," said Simms, looking up
for the first time since he entered the room. Then
he added, " You should get a stick like Rorrison's.
It has a screw handle which he keeps loose, so that
the slightest touch knocks it off. It is called the
compliment-stick, because if Rorrison is in the

company of ladies, he contrives to get them to
hold it. This is in the hope that they will knock
the handle off, when Rorrison bows and remarks
exultingly that the stick is like its owner — when
it came near them it lost its head. He has said
that to fifteen ladies now, and has a great reputation for gallantry in consequence. Good-night."

"Well, he did not get any copy out of me,"
said Rob.

"Simms is a curious fellow," Rorrison answered.
"Though you might not expect it, he has written
some of the most pathetic things I ever read, but
he wears his heart out of sight. Despite what he
says, too, he is very jealous for the Press's good
name. He seemed to take to you, so I should not
wonder though he were to look you up here some
night."

"Here? How do you mean?"

"Why, this. I shall probably be away from
London for some months, and as I must keep on
my rooms, I don't see why you should not occupy
them. The furniture is mine, and you would be
rent free, except that the housekeeper expects a
few shillings a week for looking after things. What
do you think?"

Rob could have only one thought as he compared these comfortable chambers to his own bare
room, and as Rorrison, who seemed to have taken
a warm liking to him, pressed the point, arguing

that as the rent must be paid at any rate the chambers were better occupied, he at last consented on the understanding that they could come to some arrangement on Rorrison's return.

" It will please my father, too," Rorrison added, " to know that you are here. I always remember that had it not been for him you might never have gone on to the press."

They sat so late talking this matter over that Rob eventually stayed all night, Rorrison having in his bedroom a couch which many journalists had slept on.

Next morning the paper whose nick-name is the *Scalping Knife* was served up with breakfast, and the first thing Rob saw in it was a leaderette about a disease generated in the palm of the hand by walking-sticks with heavy knobs for handles.

" I told you," said Rorrison, " that Simms would make his half-guinea out of you."

When Rorrison went down to Simms's chambers later in the day, however, to say that he was leaving Rob tenant of his rooms, he was laughing at something else.

" All during breakfast," he said to Simms, " I noticed that Angus was preoccupied, and anxious to say something that he did not like to say. At last he blurted it out with a white face, and what do you think it was ? "

Simms shook his head.

" Well," said Rorrison, " it was this. He has been accustomed to go down on his knees every night to say his prayers—as we used to do at school, but when he saw that I did not do it he did not like to do it either. I believe it troubled him all night, for he looked haggard when he rose."

" He told you this ? "

" Yes ; he said he felt ashamed of himself," said Rorrison, smiling. " You must remember he is country-bred."

" You were a good fellow, Rorrison," said Simms, gravely, " to put him into your rooms, but I don't see what you are laughing at."

" Why," said Rorrison, taken aback, " I thought you would see it in the same light."

" Not I," said Simms ; " but let me tell you this, I shall do what I can for him. I like your Angus."

CHAPTER X

Rob had a tussle for it, but he managed to live down his first winter in London, and May-day saw him sufficiently prosperous and brazen to be able to go into restaurants and shout out " Waiter." After that nothing frightened him but barmaids.

For a time his chief struggle had been with his appetite, which tortured him when he went out in the afternoons. He wanted to dine out of a paper bag, but his legs were reluctant to carry him past a grill-room. At last a compromise was agreed upon. If he got a proof over night, he dined in state next day; if it was only his manuscript that was returned to him, he thought of dining later in the week. For a long time his appetite had the worse of it. It was then that he became so great an authority on penny buns. His striking appearance always brought the saleswomen to him promptly, and sometimes he blushed, and often he glared, as he gave his order. When they smiled he changed his shop.

There was one terrible month when he wrote

165

from morning to night and did not make sixpence. He lived by selling his books, half a dozen at a time. Even on the last day of that black month he did not despair. When he wound up his watch at nights before going hungry to bed, he never remembered that it could be pawned. The very idea of entering a pawnshop never struck him. Many a time when his rejected articles came back he shook his fist in imagination at all the editors in London, and saw himself twisting their necks one by one. To think of a different death for each of them exercised his imagination and calmed his passion, and he wondered whether the murder of an editor was an indictable offence. When he did not have ten shillings, " I will get on," cried Rob to himself. " I'm not going to be starved out of a big town like this. I'll make my mark yet. Yes," he roared, while the housekeeper, at the other side of the door, quaked to hear him, " I will get on ; I'm not going to be beaten." He was waving his arms fiercely, when the housekeeper knocked. " Come in," said Rob, subsiding meekly into his chair. Before company he seemed to be without passion, but they should have seen him when he was alone. One night he dreamt that he saw all the editors in London being conveyed (in a row) to the hospital on stretchers. A gratified smile lit up his face as he slept, and his arm, going out suddenly to tip one of the stretchers over, hit against a chair. Rob jumped out of bed and kicked the chair round the room. By and by, when his articles were occasionally used, he told his proofs that the editors were capital fellows.

The only acquaintances he made were with journalists who came to his chambers to see Ror·rison, who was now in India. They seemed just as pleased to see Rob, and a few of them, who spoke largely of their connection with literature, borrowed five shillings from him. To his disappointment Noble Simms did not call, though he sometimes sent up notes to Rob suggesting likely articles, and the proper papers to which to send them. " I would gladly say 'Use my name,' " Simms wrote, " but it is the glory of anonymous journalism that names are nothing and good stuff everything. I assure you that on the press it is the men who have it in them that succeed, and the best of them become the editors." He advised Rob to go to the annual supper given by a philanthropic body to discharged criminals and write an account of the proceedings; and told him that when anything remarkable happened in London he should at once do an article (in the British Museum) on the times the same thing had happened before. " Don't neglect eclipses," he said, " nor heavy scoring at cricket matches any more than what look like signs of the times, and always try to be first in the field." He recommended Rob to gather statistics of all kinds, from the number of grandchildren the crowned heads of Europe had to the jockeys who had ridden the Derby winner more than once, and suggested the collecting of anecdotes about celebrities, which everybody would want to read if the celebrities chanced to die, as they must do some day; and he assured him that there was a public who liked to be told every year what the poets had said about May. Rob was advised never to let a historic house disappear from London without compiling an article about its associations, and to be ready to run after the fire brigade. He was told that an article on flagstone artists could be made interesting. "But always be sure of your facts," Simms said. "Write your articles over again and again, avoid fine writing as much as dishonest writing, and never spoil a leaderette by drawing it out into a leader. By and by you may be able to choose the kind of subject that interests yourself, but at present put your best work into what experienced editors believe interests the general public."

Rob found these suggestions valuable, and often thought, as he passed Simms's door, of going in to thank him, but he had an uncomfortable feeling that Simms did not want him. Of course Rob was wrong. Simms had feared at first to saddle himself with a man who might prove incapable; and besides, he generally liked those persons best whom he saw least frequently.

THE WIGWAM

For the great part of the spring Simms was out of town; but one day after his return he met Rob on the stair, and took him into his chambers. The sitting-room had been originally furnished with newspaper articles; Simms, in his younger days, when he wanted a new chair or an etching having written an article to pay for it, and then pasted the article on the back. He had paid a series on wild birds for his piano, and at one time leaderettes had even been found in the inside of his hats. Odd books and magazines lay about his table, but they would not in all have filled a library shelf; and there were no newspapers visible. The blank wall opposite the fireplace showed in dust that a large picture had recently hung there. It was an oil-painting which a month earlier had given way in the cord and fallen behind the piano, where Simms was letting it lie.

"I wonder," said Rob, who had heard from many quarters of Simms's reputation, "that you are content to put your best work into newspapers."

"Ah," answered Simms, "I was ambitious once, but, as I told you, the grand book was a failure. Nowadays I gratify myself with the reflection that I am not stupid enough ever to be a great man."

"I wish you would begin something really big," said Rob earnestly.

"I feel safer," replied Simms, "finishing something really little."

WHEN A MAN'S SINGLE

was an actor who had separated from his wife because her notices were better than his; and another
gentleman of the same profession took Rob aside
to say that he was the greatest tragedian on earth
if he could only get a chance. Rob did not know
'what to reply when the eminent cartoonist sitting
next him, whom he had looked up to for half a
dozen years, told him, by way of opening a conversation, that he had just pawned his watch.
They seemed so pleased with poverty that they
made as much of a little of it as they could, and
the wisest conclusion Rob came to that night
was not to take them too seriously. It was, however, a novel world to find oneself in all of a
sudden, one in which everybody was a wit at
his own expense. Even Simms, who always up-
held the press when any outsider ran it down, sang
with applause some verses whose point lay in their
being directed against himself. They began —

> When clever pressmen write this way,
> "As Mr. J. A. Froude would say,"
> Is it because they think he would,
> And have they read a line of Froude?
> Or is it only that they fear
> The comment they have made is queer,
> And that they either must erase it,
> Or say it's Mr. Froude who says it?

Every one abandoned himself to the humour of
the evening, and as song followed song, or was

wedged between entertainments of other kinds, the room filled with smoke until it resembled London in a fog.

By and by a sallow-faced man mounted a table to show the company how to perform a remarkable trick with three hats. He got his hats from the company, and having looked at them thoughtfully for some minutes, said that he had forgotten the way.

"That," said Simms, mentioning a well-known journalist, "is K——. He can never work unless his pockets are empty, and he would not be looking so doleful at present if he was not pretty well off. He goes from room to room in the house he lodges in, according to the state of his finances, and when you call on him you have to ask at the door which floor he is on to-day. One week you find him in the drawing-room, the next in the garret."

A stouter and brighter man followed the hat entertainment with a song, which he said was considered by some of his friends a recitation.

"There was a time," said Simms, who was held a terrible person by those who took him literally, "when that was the saddest man I knew. He was so sad that the doctors feared he would die of it. It all came of his writing for *Punch*."

"How did they treat him?" Rob asked.

"Oh, they quite gave him up, and he was wasting away visibly, when a second-rate provincial

journal appointed him its London correspondent,
and saved his life."

" Then he was sad," asked Rob, " because he
was out of work ? "

" On the contrary," said Simms, gravely, " he
was always one of the successful men, but he
could not laugh."

" And he laughed when he became a London
correspondent ? "

" Yes; that restored his sense of humour.   But
listen to this song; he is a countryman of yours
who sings it."

A man, who looked as if he had been cut out
of a granite block, and who at the end of each verse
thrust his pipe back into his mouth, sang in a broad
accent, that made Rob want to go nearer him, some
verses about an old university —

" Take off the stranger's hat ! " — The shout
 We raised in fifty-nine
Assails my ears, with careless flout,
 And now the hat is mine.
It seems a day since I was here,
 A student slim and hearty,
And see, the boys around me cheer,
 " The ancient looking party ! "

Rough horseplay did not pass for wit
 When Rae and Mill were there;
I see a lad from Oxford sit
 In Blackie's famous chair.

THE WIGWAM

And Rae, of all our men the one
    We most admired in quad
(I had this years ago), has gone
    Completely to the bad.

In our debates the moral Mill
    Had infinite address,
Alas! since then he's robbed a till,
    And now he's on the press.
And Tommy Robb, the ploughman's son,
    Whom all his fellows slighted,
From Rae and Mill the prize has won,
    For Tommy's to be knighted.

A lanky loon is in the seat
    Filled once by manse-bred Sheen,
Who did not care to mix with Peate,
    A bleacher who had been.
But watch the whirligig of time,
    Brave Peate became a preacher,
His name is known in every clime,
    And Sheen is now the bleacher.

McMillan, who the medals carried,
    Is now a judge, 't is said,
And curly-headed Smith is married,
    And Williamson is dead.
Old Phil and I who shared our books
    Now very seldom meet,
And when we do, with frowning looks
    We pass by in the street.

The college rings with student slang
    As in the days of yore,
The self-same notice boards still hang
    Upon the class-room door:

ft was thus that every one talked to Rob, who, because he took a joke without changing countenance, was considered obtuse. He congratulated one man on his articles on chaffinches in the *Evening Firebrand*, and the writer said he had discovered, since the paper appeared, that the birds he described were really linnets. Another man was introduced to Rob as the writer of " In Memoriam."

" No," said the gentleman himself, on seeing Rob start, " my name is not Tennyson. It is, indeed, Murphy. Tennyson and the other fellows, who are ambitious of literary fame, pay me so much a page for poems to which they put their names."

At this point the applause became so deafening that Simms and Rob, who had been on their way to another room, turned back. An aged man, with a magnificent head, was on his feet to describe his first meeting with Carlyle.

" Who is it ? " asked Rob, and Simms mentioned the name of a celebrity only a little less renowned than Carlyle himself. To Rob it had been one of the glories of London that in the streets he sometimes came suddenly upon world-renowned men, but he now looked upon this eminent scientist for the first time. The celebrity was there as a visitor, for the Wigwam cannot boast quite such famous members as he.

The septuagenarian began his story well. He described the approach to Craigenputtock on a warm summer afternoon, and the emotions that laid hold of him as, from a distance, he observed the sage seated astride a low dyke, flinging stones into the duck-pond. The pedestrian announced his name and the pleasure with which he at last stood face to face with the greatest writer of the day; and then the genial author of "Sartor Re, sartus," annoyed at being disturbed, jumped off the dyke and chased his visitor round and round the duck-pond. The celebrity had got thus far in his reminiscence when he suddenly stammered, bit his lip as if enraged at something, and then trembled so much that he had to be led back to his seat.

"He must be ill," whispered Rob to Simms.

"It isn't that," answered Simms; "I fancy he must have caught sight of Wingfield."

Rob's companion pointed to a melancholy-looking man in a seedy coat, who was sitting alone, glaring at the celebrity.

"Who is he?" asked Rob.

"He is the great man's literary executor," Simms replied; "come along with me and hearken to his sad tale; he is never loath to tell it."

They crossed over to Wingfield, who received them dejectedly.

"This is not a matter I care to speak of, Mr. Angus," said the sorrowful man, who spoke of it, however, as frequently as he could find a listener.

"It is now seven years since that gentleman"—
pointing angrily at the celebrity, who glared in reply—"appointed me his literary executor. At
the time I thought it a splendid appointment, and
by the end of two years I had all his remains carefully edited and his biography ready for the press.
He was an invalid at that time, supposed to be
breaking up fast; yet look at him now."

"He is quite vigorous in appearance now," said
Rob.

"Oh, I've given up hope," continued the sad
man, dolefully.

"Still," remarked Simms, "I don't know that
you could expect him to die just for your sake. I
only venture that as an opinion, of course."

"I don't ask that of him," responded Wingfield.
"I'm not blaming him in any way; all I say 's
that he has spoilt my life. Here have I been waiting, waiting for five years, and I seem further from
publication than ever."

"It is hard on you," said Simms.

"But why did he break down in his story," asked
Rob, "when he saw you?"

"Oh, the man has some sense of decency left, I
suppose, and knows that he has ruined my career."

"Is the Carlylean reminiscence taken from the
biography?" inquired Simms.

"That is the sore point," answered Wingfield,
sullenly. "He used to shun society, but now he

goes to clubs, banquets, and 'At Homes,' and tells the choice things in the memoir at every one of them. The book will scarcely be worth printing now."

"I daresay he feels sorry for you," said Simms, "and sees that he has placed you in a false position."

"He does in a way," replied the literary executor, "and yet I irritate him. When he was ill last December I called to ask for him every day, but he mistook my motives; and now he is frightened to be left alone with me."

"It is a sad business," said Simms, "but we all have our trials."

"I would try to bear up better," said the sad man, "if I got more sympathy."

It was very late when Simms and Rob left the Wigwam, yet they were amongst the first to go.

"When does the club close?" Rob asked, as they got into the fresh air.

"No one knows," answered Simms, wearily, "but I believe the last man to go takes in the morning's milk."

In the weeks that followed Rob worked hard at political articles for the *Wire*, and at last began to feel that he was making some headway. He had not the fatal facility for scribbling that distinguishes some journalists, but he had felt life before he took to writing. His style was forcible if not superfine,

creature in the street, and to have been annoyed when he discovered that a friend saw him do it. Though Simms's walls were covered with engravings Rob remembered all at once that there was not a female figure in one of them.

To sympathise with others in a love affair is delightful to every one who feels that he is all right himself. Rob went down to Simms's rooms with joyous step and a light heart. The outer door stood ajar, and as he pushed it open he heard a voice that turned his face white. From where he stood paralysed he saw through the dark passage into the sitting-room. Mary Abinger was standing before the fireplace, and as Rob's arm fell from the door, Simms bent forward and kissed her.

CHAPTER XI

ROB IS STRUCK DOWN

ROB turned from Simms's door and went quietly downstairs, looking to the beadle, who gave him a good evening at the mouth of the inn, like a man going quietly to his work. He could not keep his thoughts. They fell about him in sparks, raised by a wheel whirling so fast that it seemed motionless.

Sleep-walkers seldom come to damage until they awake; and Rob sped on, taking crossings without a halt; deaf to the shouts of cabmen, blind to their gesticulations. When you have done Oxford Circus you can do anything; but he was not even brought to himself there, though it is all savage lands in twenty square yards. For a time he saw nothing but that scene in Simms's chambers, which had been photographed on his brain. The light of his life had suddenly been turned out, leaving him only the last thing he saw to think about.

By and by he was walking more slowly, laughing at himself. Since he met Mary Abinger she had lived so much in his mind that he had not dared to

185

think of losing her. He had only given himself fits of despondency for the pleasure of dispelling them. Now all at once he saw without prejudice the Rob Angus who had made up his mind to carry off this prize, and he cut such a poor figure that he smiled grimly at it. He realized as a humorous conception that this uncouth young man who was himself must have fancied that he was, on the whole, less unworthy of Miss Abinger than were most of the young men she was likely to meet. With the exaggerated humility that comes occasionally to men in his condition, without, however, feeling sufficiently at home to remain long, he felt that there was everything in Simms a girl could find lovable, and nothing in himself. He was so terribly open that any one could understand him, while Simms was such an enigma as a girl would love to read. His own clumsiness contrasted as disastrously with Simms's grace of manner as his blunt talk compared with Simms's wit. Not being able to see himself with the eyes of others, Rob noted only one thing in his favour, his fight forward; which they, knowing, for instance, that he was better to look at than most men, would have considered his chief drawback. Rob in his calmer moments had perhaps as high an opinion of his capacity as the circumstances warranted, but he never knew that a good many ladies felt his presence when he passed them.

186

ROB IS STRUCK DOWN

Must men are hero and villain several times in a day, but Rob went through the whole gamut of sensations in half an hour, hating himself the one moment for what seemed another's fault the next, fancying now that he was blessing the union of Mary with the man she cared for, and, again, that he had Simms by the throat. He fled from the fleeting form of woman, and ran after it.

Simms had deceived him, had never even mentioned Silchester, had laughed at the awakening that was coming to him. All these months they had been waiting for Mary Abinger together, and Simms had not said that when she came it would be to him. Then Rob saw what a foolish race these thoughts ran in his brain, remembering that he had only seen Simms twice for more than a moment, and that he himself had never talked of Silchester. He scorned his own want of generosity, and recalled his solicitude for Simms's welfare an hour before.

Rob saw his whole future life lying before him. The broken-looking man with the sad face aged before his time, who walked alone up Fleet Street, was Rob Angus, who had come to London to be happy. Simms would ask him sometimes to his house to see her, but it was better that he should not go. She would understand why, if her husband did not. Her husband! Rob could not gulp down the lump in his throat. He rushed on again, with nothing before him but that picture of Simms kissing her.

Simms was not worthy of her. Why had he always seemed an unhappy, disappointed man if the one thing in the world worth striving for was his? Rob stopped abruptly in the street with the sudden thought, Was it possible that she did not care for Simms? Could that scene have had any other meaning? He had once heard Simms himself say that you never knew what a woman meant by anything until she told you, and probably not even then. But he saw again the love in her eyes as she looked up into Simms's face. All through his life he would carry that look with him.

They took no distinct shape, but wild ways of ending his misery coursed through his brain, and he looked on calmly at his own funeral. A terrible stolidity seized him, and he conceived himself a monster from whom the capacity to sympathize had gone. Children saw his face and fled from him.

He had left England far behind, and dwelt now among wild tribes who had not before looked upon a white face. Their sick came to him for miracles, and he either cured them or told them to begone. He was not sure whether he was a fiend or a missionary.

Then something remarkable happened, which showed that Rob had not mistaken his profession.

ROB IS STRUCK DOWN

He saw himself in the editorial chair that he had so often coveted, and Mary Abinger, too, was in the room. Always previously when she had come between him and the paper he had been forced to lay down his pen, but now he wrote on and on, and she seemed to help him. He was describing the scene that he had witnessed in Simms's chambers, describing it so vividly that he heard the great public discussing his article as if it were an Academy picture. His passion had subsided, and the best words formed slowly in his brain. He was hesitating about the most fitting title, when some one struck against him, and as he drew his arm over his eyes he knew with horror that he had been turning Mary Abinger into copy.

For the last time that night Rob dreamt again, and now it was such a fine picture he drew that he looked upon it with sad complacency. Many years had passed. He was now rich and famous. He passed through the wynds of Thrums, and the Auld Lichts turned out to gaze at him. He saw himself signing cheques for all kinds of charitable objects, and appearing in the subscription lists, with a grand disregard for glory that is not common to philanthropists, as X. Y. Z. or " A well-wisher." His walls were lined with books written by himself, and Mary Abinger (who had not changed in the least with the years) read them proudly, knowing that they were all written for her. (Simms

189

somehow had not fulfilled his promise.) The papers were full of his speech in the House of Commons the night before, and he had declined a seat in the Cabinet from conscientious motives. His imagination might soon have landed him master in the Mansion House, had it not deserted him when he had most need of it. He fell from his balloon like a stone. Before him he saw the blank years that had to be traversed without any Mary Abinger, and despair filled his soul. All the horrible meaning of the scene he had fled from came to him like a rush of blood to the head, and he stood with it, glaring at it, in the middle of a roaring street. Three hansoms shaved him by an inch, and the fourth knocked him senseless.

An hour later Simms was lolling in his chambers smoking, his chair tilted back until another inch would have sent him over it. His gas had been blazing all day because he had no blotting-paper, and the blinds were nicely pulled down because Mary Abinger and Nell were there to do it. They were sitting on each side of him, and Nell had on a round cap, about which Simms subsequently wrote an article. Mary's hat was larger and turned up at one side; the fashion which arose through a carriage wheel's happening to pass over the hat of a leader of fashion and make it perfectly lovely. Beyond the hats one does not care to venture, but out of fairness to Mary and Nell it should be said that there were no shiny little beads on their dresses.

They had put on their hats to go, and then they had sat down again to tell their host a great many things that they had told him already. Even Mary, who was perfect in a general sort of way, took a considerable time to tell a story, and expected it to have more point when it ended than was sometimes the case. Simms, with his eyes half closed, let the laughter ripple over his head, and drowsily heard the details of their journey from Silchester afresh. Mary had come up with the Merediths on the previous day, and they were now staying at the Langham Hotel. They would only be in town for a few weeks; "just to oblige the season," Nell said, for she had inveigled her father into taking a houseboat on the Thames, and was certain it would prove delightful. Mary was to accompany them there too, having first done her duty to society, and Colonel Abinger was setting off shortly for the continent. In the middle of her prattle, Nell distinctly saw Simms's head nod, as if it was loose in its socket. She made a mournful grimace.

Simms sat up.

"Your voices did it," he explained, unabashed. "They are as soothing to the jaded journalist as the streams that murmur through the fields in June."

"Cigars are making you stupid, Dick," said Mary; "I do wonder why men smoke."

"I have often asked myself that question," thoughtfully answered Simms, whom it is time to call by his real name of Dick Abinger. "I know some men who smoke because they might get sick otherwise when in the company of smokers. Others smoke because they began to do so at school, and are now afraid to leave off. A great many men smoke for philanthropic motives, smoking enabling them to work harder, and so being for their family's good. At picnics men smoke because it is the only way to keep the midges off the ladies. Smoking keeps you cool in summer and warm in winter, and is an excellent disinfectant. There are even said to be men who admit that they smoke because they like it, but for my own part I fancy I smoke because I forget not to do so."

"Silly reason," said Nell. If there was one possible improvement she could conceive in Dick, it was that he might make his jests a little easier.

"It is revealing no secret," murmured Abinger in reply, "to say that drowning men clutch at straws."

Mary rose to go once more, and sat down again, for she had remembered something else.

"Do you know, Dick," she said, "that your two names are a great nuisance. On our way to London yesterday there was an acquaintance of Mr. Meredith's in the carriage, and he told us he knew Noble Simms well."

"Yes," said Nell, "and that this Noble Simms was an old gentleman who had been married for thirty years. We said we knew Mr. Noble Simms, and that he was a barrister, and he laughed at us. So you see some one is trading on your name."

"Much good may it do him," said Abinger, generously.

"But it is horrid," said Nell, "that we should have to listen to people praising Noble Simms's writings, and not be allowed to say that he is Dick Abinger in disguise."

"It must be very hard on you, Nell, to have to keep a secret," admitted Dick, "but you see I must lead two lives or be undone. In the Temple you will see the name of Richard Abinger, barrister-at-law, but in Frobisher's Inn he is J. Noble Simms."

"I don't see the good of it," said Nell.

"My ambition, you must remember," explained Dick, "is to be Lord Chancellor or Lord Chief Justice, I forget which, but while I wait for that post I must live, and I live by writings (which are all dead the morning after they appear). Now such is the suspicion with which literature is regarded by the legal mind that were it known I wrote for the press my chance of the Lord Chancellorship would cease to be a moral certainty. The editor of the *Scalping Knife* has not the least notion that Noble Simms is the rising barrister who has been known to make as much by the law as a guinea in a single month. Indeed, only my most intimate friends, some of whom practise the same deception themselves, are aware that the singular gifts of Simms and Abinger are united in the same person."

"The housekeeper here must know?" asked Mary.

"No, it would hopelessly puzzle her," said Dick; "she would think there was something uncanny about it, and so she is happy in the belief that the letters which occasionally come addressed to Abinger are forwarded by me to that gentleman's abode in the Temple."

"It is such an ugly name, Noble Simms," said Nell; "I wonder why you selected it."

"It is ugly, is it not?" said Dick. "It struck me at the time as the most ridiculous name I was likely to think of, and so I chose it. Such a remarkable name sticks to the public mind, and that is fame."

As he spoke he rose to get the two girls the cab that would take them back to the hotel.

"There is some one knocking at the door," said Mary.

"Come in," murmured Abinger.

The housekeeper opened the door, but half shut it again when she saw that Dick was not alone. Then she thought of a compromise between telling her business and retiring.

"If you please, Mr. Simms," she said, apologetically, " would you speak to me a moment in the passage ? "

Abinger disappeared with her, and when he returned the indifferent look had gone from his face.

" Wait for me a few minutes," he said ; " a man upstairs, one of the best fellows breathing, has met with an accident, and I question if he has a friend in London. I am going up to see him."

" Poor fellow ! " said Mary to Nell, after Dick had gone ; " fancy his lying here for weeks without any one's going near him but Dick."

" But how much worse it would be without Dick ! " said Nell.

" I wonder if he is a barrister," said Mary.

" I think he will be a journalist rather," Nell said, thoughtfully, " a tall, dark, melancholy-look-ing man, and I should not wonder though he had a broken heart."

" I'm afraid it is more serious than that," said Mary.

Nell set off on a trip round the room, remarking with a profound sigh that it must be awful to live alone and have no one to speak to for whole hours at a time. " I should go mad," she said, in such a tone of conviction that Mary did not think of questioning it.

Then Nell, who had opened a drawer rather guiltily, exclaimed, " Oh, Mary ! "

WHEN A MAN'S SINGLE

A woman can put more meaning into a note of exclamation than a man can pack in a sentence. It costs Mr. Jones, for instance, a long message simply to telegraph to his wife that he is bringing a friend home to dinner, but in a sixpenny reply Mrs. Jones can warn him that he had better do no such thing, that he ought to be ashamed of himself for thinking of it, that he must make some excuse to his friend, and that he will hear more of this when he gets home. Nell's " Oh, Mary ! " signified that chaos was come.

Mary hastened round the table, and found her friend with a letter in her hand.

" Well," said Mary, " that is one of your letters to Dick, is it not ? "

" Yes," answered Nell, tragically ; " but fancy his keeping my letters lying about carelessly in a drawer — and — and, yes, using them as scribbling paper ! "

Scrawled across the envelopes in a barely decipherable handwriting were such notes as these : " Schoolboys smoking master's cane-chair, work up ; " " Return of the swallows (poetic or humorous ?) ; " " My First Murder (magazine ?) ; " " Better do something pathetic for a change."

There were tears in Nell's eyes.

" This comes of prying," said Mary.

" Oh, I wasn't prying," said Nell ; " I only opened it by accident. That is the worst of it. I can't say anything about them to him, because he might think I had opened his drawer to — to see what was in it — which is the last thing in the world I would think of doing. Oh, Mary," she added, woefully, "what do you think ? "

" I think you are a goose," said Mary, promptly.

" Ah, you are so indifferent," Nell said, surrendering her position all at once. "Now when I see a drawer I am quite unhappy until I know what is in it, especially if it is locked. When we lived opposite the Burtons I was miserable because they always kept the blind of one of their windows down. If I had been a boy I would have climbed up to see why they did it. Ah! that is Dick; I know his step."

She was hastening to the door, when she remembered the letters, and subsided primly into a chair.

" Well ? " asked Mary, as her brother re-entered with something in his hand.

" The poor fellow has had a nasty accident," said Dick; "run over in the street, it seems. He ought to have been taken to the infirmary, but they got a letter with his address on it in his pocket, and brought him here."

" Has a doctor seen him ? "

" Yes, but I hardly make out from the housekeeper what he said. He was gone before I went up. There are some signs, however, of what he did. The poor fellow seems to have been struck on the head."

Mary shuddered, understanding that some operation had been found necessary.

"Did he speak to you?" asked Nell.

"He was asleep," said Dick, "but talking more than he does when he is awake."

"He must have been delirious," said Mary.

"One thing I can't make out," Dick said, more to himself than to his companions. "He mumbled my name to himself half a dozen times while I was upstairs."

"But is there anything remarkable in that," asked Mary, "if he has so few friends in London?"

"What I don't understand," explained Dick, "is that the word I caught was Abinger. Now, I am quite certain that he only knew me as Noble Simms."

"Some one must have told him your real name," said Mary. "Is he asleep now?"

"That reminds me of another thing," said Dick, looking at the torn card in his hand. "Just as I was coming away he staggered off the couch where he is lying to his desk, opened it, and took out this card. He glared at it, and tore it in two before I got him back to the couch.

There were tears in Nell's eyes now, for she felt that she understood it all.

"It is horrible to think of him alone up there," she cried. "Let us go up to him, Mary."

Mary hesitated.

"I don't think it would be the thing," she said, taking the card from Nell's hand. She started slightly as she looked at it, and then became white.

"What is his name, Dick?" she faltered, in a voice that made Nell look at her.

"Angus," said Dick. "He has been on the press here for some months."

The name suggested nothing at the moment to Nell, but Mary let the card fall. It was a shabby little Christmas card.

"I think we should go up and see if we can do anything," Dick's sister said.

"But would it be the thing?" Nell asked.

"Of course, it would," said Mary, a little sur-prised at Nell.

CHAPTER XII

THE STUPID SEX

Give a man his chance, and he has sufficient hardihood for anything. Within a week of the accident Rob was in Dick Abinger's most luxurious chair, coolly taking a cup and saucer from Nell, while Mary arranged a cushion for his poor head. He even made several light-hearted jests, at which his nurses laughed heartily — because he was an invalid.

Rob's improvement dated from the moment he opened his eyes, and heard the soft rustle of a lady's skirts in the next room. He lay quietly listening, and realized by and by that he had known she was Mary Abinger all along.

" Who is that ? " he said, abruptly, to Dick, who was swinging his legs on the dressing-table. Dick came to him as awkwardly as if he had been asked to hold a baby, and saw no way of getting out of it. Sick-rooms chilled him.

" Are you feeling better now, old fellow ? " he asked.

" Who is it ? " Rob repeated, sitting up in bed.

" That is my sister," Dick said.

Rob's head fell back. He could not take it in all at once. Dick thought he had fallen asleep, and tried to slip gently from the room, discovering for the first time as he did so that his shoes creaked.

"Don't go," said Rob, sitting up again. "What is your sister's name?"

"Abinger, of course, Mary Abinger," answered Dick, under the conviction that the invalid was still off his head. He made for the door again, but Rob's arm went out suddenly and seized him.

"You are a liar, you know," Rob said, feebly; "she's not your sister."

"No, of course not," said Dick, humouring him.

"I want to see her," Rob said, authoritatively.

"Certainly," answered Dick, escaping into the other room, to tell Mary that the patient was raving again.

"I heard him," said Mary.

"Well, what's to be done?" asked her brother. "He's madder than ever."

"Oh no, I think he's getting on nicely now," Mary said, moving toward the bedroom.

"Don't," exclaimed Dick, getting in front of her; "why, I tell you his mind is wandering. He says you're not my sister."

"Of course he can't understand so long as he thinks your name is Simms."

"But he knows my name is Abinger. Didn't I tell you I heard him groaning it over to himself?"

"Oh, Dick," said Mary, "I wish you would go away and write a stupid article."

Dick, however, stood at the door, ready to come to his sister's assistance if Rob got violent.

"He says you are his sister," said the patient to Mary.

"So I am," said Mary, softly. "My brother writes under the name of Noble Simms, but his real name is Abinger. Now you must lie still and think about that; you are not to talk any more."

"I won't talk any more," said Rob, slowly. "You are not going away, though?"

"Just for a little while," Mary answered. "The doctor will be here presently."

"Well, you have quieted him," Dick admitted.

They were leaving the room, when they heard Rob calling.

"There he goes again," said Dick, groaning.

"What is it?" Mary asked, returning to the bedroom.

"Why did he say you were not his sister?" Rob said, very suspiciously.

"Oh, his mind was wandering," Mary answered, cruelly.

She was retiring again, but stopped undecidedly. Then she looked from the door to see if her brother was within hearing. Dick was at the other end of the sitting-room, and she came back noiselessly to Rob's bedside.

THE STUPID SEX

"Do you remember," she asked, in a low voice, "how the accident happened? You know you were struck by a cab."

"Yes," answered Rob at once, "I saw him kissing you. I don't remember anything after that."

Mary, looking like a culprit, glanced hurriedly at the door. Then she softly pushed the invalid's unruly hair off his brow, and glided from the room smiling.

"Well?" asked Dick.

"He was telling me how the accident happened," Mary said.

"And how was it?"

"Oh, just as you said. He got bewildered at a crossing, and was knocked over."

"But he wasn't the man to lose his reason at a crossing," said Dick. "There must have been something to agitate him."

"He said nothing about that," replied Mary, without blushing.

"Did he tell you how he knew my name was Abinger?" Dick asked, as they went downstairs.

"No," his sister said, "I forgot to ask him."

"There was that Christmas card, too," Dick said, suddenly. "Nell says Angus must be in love, poor fellow."

"Nell is always thinking people are in love," Mary answered, severely.

"By the way," said Dick, "what became of the card? He might want to treasure it, you know."

"I — I rather think I put it somewhere," Mary said.

"I wonder," Dick remarked, curiously, "what sort of girl Angus would take to?"

"I wonder," said Mary.

They were back in Dick's chambers by this time, and he continued with some complacency — for all men think they are on safe ground when discussing an affair of the heart: —

"We could build the young lady up from the card, which, presumably, was her Christmas offering to him. It was not expensive, so she is a careful young person; and the somewhat florid design represents a blue bird sitting on a pink twig, so that we may hazard the assertion that her artistic taste is not as yet fully developed. She is a fresh country maid, or the somewhat rich colouring would not have taken her fancy, and she is short, a trifle stout, or a big man like Angus would not have fallen in love with her. Reserved men like gushing girls, so she gushes and says 'Oh my!' and her nicest dress (here Dick shivered) is of a shiny satin with a dash of rich velvet here and there. Do you follow me?"

"Yes," said Mary; "it is wonderful. I suppose, now, you are never wrong when you 'build up' so much on so little?"

"Sometimes we go a little astray," admitted Dick. "I remember going into a hotel with Rorrison once, and on a table we saw a sailor-hat lying, something like the one Nell wears — or is it you?"

"The idea of your not knowing!" said his sister, indignantly.

"Well, we discussed the probable owner. I concluded, after narrowly examining the hat, that she was tall, dark, and handsome, rather than pretty. Rorrison, on the other hand, maintained that she was a pretty, baby-faced girl, with winning ways."

"And did you discover if either of you was right?"

"Yes," said Dick, slowly. "In the middle of the discussion a little boy in a velvet suit toddled into the room, and said to us, 'Gim'me my hat.'"

In the weeks that followed, Rob had many delicious experiences. He was present at several tea-parties in Abinger's chambers, the guests being strictly limited to three; and when he could not pretend to be ill any longer, he gave a tea-party himself in honour of his two nurses — his one and a half nurses, Dick called them. At this Mary poured out the tea, and Rob's eyes showed so plainly (though not to Dick) that he had never seen anything like it, that Nell became thoughtful, and made a number of remarks on the subject to her mother as soon as she returned home.

"It would never do," Nell said, looking wise.

"Whatever would the colonel say!" exclaimed Mrs. Meredith. "After all, though," she added — for she had been to see Rob twice, and liked him because of something he had said to her about his mother — "he is just the same as Richard."

"Oh no, no," said Nell, "Dick is an Oxford man, you must remember, and Mr. Angus, as the colonel would say, rose from obscurity."

"Well, if he did," persisted Mrs. Meredith, "he does not seem to be going back to it, and universities seem to me to be places for making young men stupid."

"It would never, never do," said Nell, with doleful decision.

"What does Mary say about him?" asked her mother.

"She never says anything," said Nell.

"Does she talk much to him?"

"No; very little."

"That is a good sign," said Mrs. Meredith.

"I don't know," said Nell.

"Have you noticed anything else?"

"Nothing except — well, Mary is longer in dressing now than I am, and she used not to be."

"I wonder," Mrs. Meredith remarked, "if Mary saw him at Silchester after that time at the Castle?"

"She never told me she did," Nell answered,

"but sometimes I think — however, there is no good in thinking."

"It isn't a thing you often do, Nell. By the way, he saw the first Sir Clement at Dome Castle, did he not?"

"Yes," Nell said, "he saw the impostor, and I don't suppose he knows there is another Sir Clement. The Abingers don't like to speak of that. However, they may meet on Friday, for Dick has got Mr. Angus a card for the Symphonia, and Sir Clement is to be there."

"What does Richard say about it?" asked Mrs. Meredith, going back apparently upon their conversation.

"We never speak about it, Dick and I," said Nell.

"What do you speak about, then?"

"Oh, nothing," said Nell.

Mrs. Meredith sighed.

"And you such an heiress, Nell," she said; "you could do so much better. He will never have anything but what he makes by writing; and if all stories be true, half of that goes to the colonel. I'm sure your father never will consent."

"Oh yes, he will," Nell said.

"If he had really tried to get on at the bar," Mrs. Meredith pursued, "it would not have been so bad, but he is evidently to be a newspaper man all his life."

"I wish you would say journalist, mamma," Nell said, pouting, " or literary man. The profession of letters is a noble one."

" Perhaps it is," Mrs. Meredith assented, with another sigh, " and I daresay he told you so, but I can't think it is very respectable."

Rob did not altogether enjoy the Symphonia, which is a polite 'club attended by the literary fry of both sexes; the ladies who write because they cannot help it, the poets who excuse their verses because they were young when they did them, the clergymen who publish their sermons by request of their congregations, the tourists who have been to Spain and cannot keep it to themselves. The club meets once a fortnight, for the purpose of not listening to music and recitations; and the members, of whom the ladies outnumber the men, sit in groups round little lions who roar mildly. The Symphonia is very fashionable and select, and having heard the little lions a-roaring, you get a cup of coffee and go home again.

Dick explained that he was a member of the Symphonia because he rather liked to put on the lion's skin himself now and again, and he took Mrs. Meredith and the two girls to it to show them of what literature in its higher branches is capable. The elegant dresses of the literary ladies, and the suave manner of the literary gentlemen, impressed Nell's mother favourably, and the Symphonia, which she had taken for an out-at-elbows club, raised letters in her estimation.

Rob, however, who never felt quite comfortable in evening dress, had a bad time of it, for Dick carried him off at once, and got him into a group round the authoress of " My Baby Boy," to whom Rob was introduced as a passionate admirer of her delightful works. The lion made room for him, and he sat sadly beside her, wishing he was not so big.

Both of the rooms of the Symphonia club were crowded, but a number of gentlemen managed to wander, from group to group over the skirts of ladies' gowns. Rob watched them wistfully from his cage, and observed one come to rest at the back of Mary Abinger's chair. He was a medium-sized man, and for five minutes Rob thought he was Sir Clement Dowton. Then he realized that he had been deceived by a remarkable resemblance.

The stranger said a great deal to Mary, and she seemed to like him. After a long time the authoress's voice broke in on Rob's cogitations, and when he saw that she was still talking without looking tired, a certain awe filled him. Then Mary rose from her chair, taking the arm of the gentleman who was Sir Clement's double, and they went into the other room, where the coffee was served.

Rob was tempted to sit there stupidly miserable, for the easiest thing to do comes to us first. Then he thought it was better to be a man, and, drawing up his chest, boldly asked the lion to have a cup of coffee. In another moment he was steering her through the crowd, her hand resting on his arm, and, to his amazement, he found he rather liked it.

In the coffee-room Rob could not distinguish the young lady who moved like a swan, but he was elated with his social triumph, and cast about for any journalist of his acquaintance who, he thought, might like to meet the authoress of "My Baby Boy." It struck Rob that he had no right to keep her all to himself. Quite close to him his eye lighted on Marriott, the author of "Mary Hooney: a Romance of the Irish Question," but Marriott saw what he was after, and dived into the crowd. A very young gentleman with large empty eyes, begged Rob's pardon for treading on his toes, and Rob, who had not felt it, saw that this was his man. He introduced him to the authoress as another admirer, and the round-faced youth seemed such a likely subject for her next work that Rob moved off comfortably.

A shock awaited him when he met Dick, who had been passing the time by taking male guests aside and asking them in an impressive voice what they thought of his great book, "Lives of Eminent Washerwomen," which they had no doubt read.

"Who is the man so like Dowton?" he repeated, in answer to Rob's question. "Why, it is Dowton."

THE STUPID SEX

Then Dick looked vexed. He remembered that Rob had been at Dome Castle on the previous Christmas Eve.

"Look here, Angus," he said, bluntly, "this is a matter I hate to talk about. The fact is, however, that this is the real Sir Clement. The fellow you met was an impostor, who came from no one knows where. Unfortunately, he has returned to the same place."

Dick bit his lip while Rob digested this.

"But if you know the real Dowton," Rob asked, "how were you deceived?"

"Well, it was my father who was deceived rather than myself, but we did not know the real baronet then. The other fellow, if you must know, traded on his likeness to Dowton, who is in the country now for the first time for many years. Whoever the impostor is, he is a humourist in his way, for when he left the Castle in January he asked my father to call on him when he came to town. The fellow must have known that Dowton was coming home about that time; at all events, my father, who was in London shortly afterwards, looked up his friend the baronet, as he thought, at his club, and found that he had never set eyes on him before. It would make a delicious article if it had not happened in one's own family."

"The real Sir Clement seems great friends with Miss Abinger." Rob could not help saying.

"Yes," said Dick, "we struck up an intimacy with him over the affair, and stranger things have happened than that he and Mary — "

He stopped.

"My father, I believe, would like it," he added, carelessly, but Rob had turned away. Dick went after him.

"I have told you this," he said, "because, as you knew the other man, it had to be done, but we don't like it spoken of."

"I shall not speak of it," said miserable Rob.

He would have liked to be tearing through London again, but as that was not possible he sought a solitary seat by the door. Before he reached it his mood changed. What was Sir Clement Dowton, after all, that he should be frightened at him? He was merely a baronet. An impostor who could never have passed for a journalist had succeeded in passing for Dowton. Journalism was the noblest of all professions, and Rob was there representing it. The seat of honour at the Symphonia was next to Mary Abinger, and the baronet had held it too long already. Instead of sulking, Rob approached the throne like one who had a right to be there. Sir Clement had risen for a moment to put down Mary's cup, and when he returned Rob was in his chair, with no immediate intention of getting out of it. The baronet frowned, which made Rob say quite a number of bright things to Miss Abinger. When two men are in love with the same young lady one of them must be worsted. Rob saw that it was better to be the other one.

The frightfully Bohemian people at the Symphonia remained there even later than eleven o'clock, but the rooms thinned before then, and Dick's party were ready to go by half-past ten. Rob was now very sharp. It did not escape his notice that the gentlemen were bringing the ladies' cloaks, and he calmly made up his mind to help Mary Abinger on with hers. To his annoyance, Sir Clement was too quick for him. The baronet was in the midst of them, with the three ladies' cloaks, just as Rob wondered where he would have to go to find them. Nell's cloak Sir Clement handed to Dick, but he kept Mary's on his arm while he assisted Mrs. Meredith into hers. It was a critical moment. All would be over in five seconds.

"Allow me," said Rob.

With apparent coolness he took Mary's cloak from the baronet's arms. He had not been used to saying "allow me," and his face was white, but he was determined to go on with this thing.

"Take my arm," he said to Mary, as they joined the crowd that swayed toward the door. After he said it he saw that he had spoken with an air of proprietorship, but he was not sorry. Mary did it.

It took them some time to reach their cab, and on the way Mary asked Rob a question.

"I gave you something once," she said, "but I suppose you lost it long ago."

Rob reddened, for he had been sadly puzzled to know what had become of his Christmas card.

"I have it still," he answered at last.

"Oh," said Mary, coldly; and at once Rob felt a chill pass through him. It was true, after all, that Miss Abinger could be an icicle on occasion.

Rob, having told a lie, deserved no mercy, and got none. The pity of it is that Mary might have thawed a little had she known that it was only a lie. She thought that Rob was not aware of his loss. A man taking fickleness as the comparative degree of an untruth is perhaps only what may be looked for, but one does not expect it from a woman. Probably the lights had blinded Mary.

Rob had still an opportunity of righting himself, but he did not take it.

"Then you did mean the card for me," he said, in foolish exultation; "when I found it on the walk I was not certain that you had not merely dropped it by accident."

Alas! for the fatuity of man. Mary looked up in icy surprise.

"What card?" she said. "I don't know what you are talking about."

214

"Don't you remember?" asked Rob, very much requiring to be sharpened again.

He looked so woebegone, that Mary nearly had pity on him. She knew, however, that, if it was not for her sex, men would never learn anything.

"No," she replied, and turned to talk to Sir Clement.

Rob walked home from the Langham that night with Dick, and, when he was not thinking of the two Sir Clements, he was telling himself that he had climbed his hill valiantly, only to topple over when he neared the top. Before he went to bed he had an article to finish for the *Wire*, and, while he wrote, he pondered over the ways of woman; which, when you come to think of it, is a droll thing to do.

Mr. Meredith had noticed Rob's dejection at the hotel, and remarked to Nell's mother that he thought Mary was very stiff to Angus. Mrs. Meredith looked sadly at her husband in reply.

"You think so," she said, mournfully shaking her head at him, "and so does Richard Abinger. Mr. Angus is as blind as the rest of you."

"I don't understand," said Mr. Meredith, with much curiosity.

"Nor do they," replied his wife, contemptuously; "there are no men so stupid, I think, as the clever ones."

She could have preached a sermon that night, with the stupid sex for her text.

CHAPTER XIII

THE HOUSEBOAT, "TAWNY OWL"

"MR. ANGUS, what is an egotist?"

"Don't you know, Miss Meredith?"

"Well, I know in a general sort of way, but not precisely."

"An egotist is a person who — but why do *you* want to know?"

"Because just now Mr. Abinger asked me what I was thinking of, and when I said of nothing he called me an egotist."

"Ah! that kind of egotist is one whose thoughts are too deep for utterance."

It was twilight. Rob stood on the deck of the houseboat, *Tawny Owl*, looking down at Nell, who sat in the stern, her mother beside her, amid a blaze of Chinese lanterns. Dick lay near them, prone, as he had fallen from a hammock whose one flaw was that it gave way when any one got into it. Mr. Meredith, looking out from one of the saloon windows across the black water that was now streaked with glistening silver, wondered whether he was enjoying himself, and Mary, in a little blue nautical jacket with a cap to match, lay back in a camp-chair on deck with a silent banjo in her hands. Rob was brazening it out in flannels, and had been at such pains to select colours to suit him that the effect was atrocious. He had spent several afternoons at Molesey during the three weeks the *Tawny Owl* had lain there, but this time he was to remain overnight at the Island Hotel.

The *Tawny Owl* was part of the hoop of houseboats that almost girded Tagg's Island, and lights sailed through the trees, telling of launches moving to their moorings near the ferry. Now and again there was the echo of music from a distant houseboat. For a moment the water was loquacious as dingeys or punts shot past. Canadian canoes, the ghosts that haunt the Thames by night, lifted their heads out of the river, gaped, and were gone. An osier wand dipped into the water under a weight of swallows, all going to bed together. The boy on the next houseboat kissed his hand to a broom on board the *Tawny Owl*, taking it for Mrs. Meredith's servant, and then retired to his kitchen smiling. From the boathouse across the river came the monotonous tap of a hammer. A reed-warbler rushed through his song. There was a soft splashing along the bank.

"There was once a literary character," Dick murmured, "who said that to think of nothing was an impossibility, but he lived before the days of house-

WHEN A MAN'S SINGLE

But Coelebs now has slothful grown
    (I learn this from her mother),
Instead of making her his own,
    He asks to be her brother.

Last night I saw her smooth his brow,
    He bent his head and kissed her;
They understand each other now,
    She's going to be his sister.
Some say he really does propose,
    And means to gain or lose all,
And that the new arrangement goes,
    To soften her refusal.

H ˜ talks so wild of broken heart,
    Of futures that she'll mar,
He says on Tuesday he departs
    For Cork or Zanzibar.
His death he places at her door,
    Yet says he won't resent it;
Ah, well, he talked that way before,
    And very seldom meant it.

Engagements now are curious things,
    " A kind of understandin'."
Although they do not run to rings,
    They're good to keep your hand in.
No rivals now, Tom, Dick and Hal,
    They all love one another,
For she's a sister to them all,
    And every one's her brother.

In former days when men proposed,
    And ladies said them No,
The laws that courtesy imposed
    Made lovers pack and go.

But now that they may brothers be,
  So changed the way of men is,
That, having kissed, the swain and she
  Resume their game at tennis.

Ah, Nelly Meredith, you may
  Be wiser than your mother,
But she knew what to do when they
  Proposed to be her brother.
Of these relations best have none,
  They'll only you encumber;
Of wives a man may have but one,
  Of sisters any number.

Dick disappeared into the kitchen with Mrs.
Meredith, to show her how they make a salad at
the Wigwam, and Nell and her father went a fishing from a bedroom window. The night was so
silent now that Rob and Mary seemed to have it
to themselves. A canoe in a blaze of coloured
light drifted past without a sound. The grass on
the bank parted, and water-rats peeped out. All ·
at once Mary had nothing to say, and Rob shook
on his stool. The moon was out looking at them.

"Oh," Mary cried, as something dipped suddenly in the water near them.

"It was only a dabchick," Rob guessed, looking
over the rail.

"What is a dabchick?" asked Mary.

Rob did not tell her. She had not the least
desire to know.

In the river, on the opposite side from where the *Tawny Owl* lay, a stream drowns itself. They had not known of its existence before, but it was roaring like a lasher to them now. Mary shuddered slightly, turning her face to the island, and Rob took a great breath as he looked at her. His hand held her brown sunshade that was ribbed with velvet, the sunshade with the preposterous handle that Mary held upside down. Other ladies carried their sunshades so, and Rob resented it. Her back was toward him, and he sat still, gazing at the loose blue jacket that only reached her waist. It was such a slender waist that Rob trembled for it.

The trees that hung over the houseboat were black, but the moon made a fairyland of the sward beyond. Mary could only see the island between heavy branches, but she looked straight before her until tears dimmed her eyes. Who would dare to seek the thoughts of a girl at such a moment? Rob moved nearer her. Her blue cap was tilted back, her chin rested on the rail. All that was good in him was astir when she turned and read his face.

"I think I shall go down now," Mary said, becoming less pale as she spoke. Rob's eyes followed her as she moved toward the ladder.

"Not yet," he called after her, and could say no more. It was always so when they were alone; and he made himself suffer for it afterwards.

Mary stood irresolutely at the top of the ladder.

She would not turn back, but she did not descend.
Mr. Meredith was fishing lazily from the lower
deck, and there was a murmur of voices in the
saloon. On the road running parallel to the river
traps and men were shadows creeping along to
Hampton. Lights were going out there. Mary
looked up the stretch of water and sighed.

"Was there ever so beautiful a night?" she
said.

"Yes," said Rob, at her elbow, "once at Dome
Castle, the night I saw you first."

"I don't remember," said Mary hastily, but
without going down the ladder.

"I might never have met you," Rob continued,
grimly, "if some man in Silchester had not mur-
dered his wife."

Mary started and looked up at him. Until she
ceased to look he could not go on.

"The murder," he explained, "was of more im-
portance than Colonel Abinger's dinner, and so I
was sent to the castle. It is rather curious to trace
these things back a step. The woman enraged her
husband into striking her, because she had not prepared his supper. Instead of doing that she had
been gossiping with a neighbour, who would not
have had time for gossip had she not been laid up
with a sprained ankle. It came out in the evi-
dence that this woman had hurt herself by slipping
on a marble, so that I might never have seen you

had not two boys, whom neither of us ever heard of, challenged each other to a game at marbles."

"It was stranger that we should meet again in London," Mary said.

"No," Rob answered, "the way we met was strange, but I was expecting you."

Mary pondered how she should take this, and then pretended not to hear it.

"Was it not rather 'The Scorn of Scorns' that made us know each other?" she asked.

"I knew you after I read it a second time," he said; "I have got that copy of it still."

"You said you had the card."

"I have never been able to understand," Rob answered, "how I lost that card. But," he added, sharply, "how do you know that I lost it?"

Mary glanced up again.

"I hate being asked questions, Mr. Angus," she said, sweetly.

"Do you remember," Rob went on, "saying in that book that men were not to be trusted until they reached their second childhood?"

"I don't know," Mary replied, laughing, "that they are to be trusted even then."

"I should think," said Rob, rather anxiously, "that a woman might as well marry a man in his first childhood as in his second. Surely the golden mean —" Rob paused. He was just twenty-seven.

"We should strike the golden mean, you think?" asked Mary, demurely. "But you see it is of such short duration."

After that there was such a long pause that Mary could easily have gone down the ladder had she wanted to do so.

"I am glad that you and Dick are such friends," she said at last.

"Why?" asked Rob, quickly.

"Oh, well," said Mary.

"He has been the best friend I have ever made," Rob continued, warmly, "though he says our only point in common is a hatred of rice pudding."

"He told me," said Mary, "that you write on politics in the *Wire*."

"I do a little now, but I have never met any one yet who admitted that he had read my articles. Even your brother won't go so far as that."

"I have read several of them," said Mary.

"Have you?" Rob exclaimed, like a big boy.

"Yes," Mary answered severely: "but I don't agree with them. I am a Conservative, you know."

She pursed up her mouth complacently as she spoke, and Rob fell back a step to prevent his going a step closer. He could hear Mr. Meredith's line tearing the water. The boy on the next houseboat was baling the dingey, and whistling a doleful ditty between each canful.

" There will never be such a night again," Rob
said, in a melancholy voice. Then he waited for
Mary to ask why, when he would have told her,
but she did not ask.

"At least, not to me," he continued, after a
pause, "for I am not likely to be here again. But
there may be many such nights to you."

Mary was unbuttoning her gloves and then buttoning them again. There is something uncanny
about a woman who has a chance to speak and
does not take it.

"I am glad to hear," said Rob, "that my being
away will make no difference to you."

A light was running along the road to Hampton
Court, and Mary watched it.

"Are you glad?" asked Rob, desperately.

"You said I was," answered Mary, without turning her head. Dick was thrumming the banjo
below. Her hand touched a camp-chair, and Rob
put his over it. He would have liked to stand
like that and talk about things in general now.

"Mary," said Rob.

The boy ceased to whistle. All nature in that
quarter was paralysed, except the tumble of water
across the river. Mary withdrew her hand, but
said nothing. Rob held his breath. He had not
even the excuse of having spoken impulsively, for
he had been meditating saying it for weeks.

By and by the world began to move again. The

boy whistled. A swallow tried another twig. A moorhen splashed in the river. They had thought it over, and meant to let it pass.

"Are you angry with me?" Rob asked.

Mary nodded her head, but did not speak. Suddenly Rob started.

"You are crying," he said.

"No, I'm not," said Mary, looking up now.

There was a strange light in her face that made Rob shake. He was so near her that his hands touched her jacket. At that moment there was a sound of feet on the plank that communicated between the *Tawny Owl* and the island, and Dick called out —

"You people up there, are you coming once around the island before you have something to eat?"

Rob muttered a reply that Dick fortunately did not catch, but Mary answered "Yes," and they descended the ladder.

"You had better put a shawl over your shoulders," said Rob, in rather a lordly tone.

"No," Mary answered, thrusting away the shawl he produced from the saloon; "a wrap on a night like this would be absurd."

Something caught in her throat at that moment, and she coughed. Rob looked at her anxiously.

"You had better," he said, putting the shawl over her shoulders.

227

" No," said Mary, flinging it off.

" Yes," said Rob, putting it on again.

Mary stamped her foot.

" How dare you, Mr. Angus ? " she exclaimed.

Rob's chest heaved.

" You must do as you are told," he said.

Mary looked at him while he looked at her, but she did not take off the shawl again, and that was the great moment of Rob's life.

The others had gone on before. Although it was a white night the plank was dark in shadow, and as she stepped off it she slipped back. Rob's arm went round her for a moment. They walked round the island together behind the others, but neither uttered a word. Rob was afraid even to look at her, so he did not see that Mary looked once or twice at him.

Long after he was supposed to be in the hotel Rob was still walking round the island, with no one to see him but the cow. All the Chinese lanterns were out now, but red window blinds shone warm in several houseboats, and a terrier barked at his footsteps. The grass was silver-tipped, as in an enchanted island, and the impatient fairies might only have been waiting till he was gone. He was wondering if she was offended. While he paced the island she might be vowing never to look at him again, but perhaps she was only thinking that he was very much improved.

THE HOUSEBOAT, "TAWNY OWL"

At last Rob wandered to the hotel, and reaching his bedroom sat down on a chair to think it out again by candle light. He rose and opened the window. There was a notice over the mantelpiece announcing that smoking was not allowed in the bedrooms, and having read it thoughtfully he filled his pipe. A piece of crumpled paper lay beneath the dressing-table, and he lifted it up to make a spill of it. It was part of an envelope, and it floated out of Rob's hand as he read the address in Mary Abinger's handwriting, " Sir Clement Dowton, Island Hotel."

CHAPTER XIV

MARY OF THE STONY HEART

A PUNT and a rowing-boat were racing lazily toward Sunbury on a day so bright that you might have passed women with their hair in long curls and forgiven them.

" I say, Dick," said one of the scullers, " are they engaged ? "

Will was the speaker, and in asking the question he caught a crab. Mary, with her yellow sleeves turned up at the wrist, a great straw hat on her head, ran gaily after her pole, and the punt jerked past. If there are any plain girls let them take to punting and be beautiful.

Dick, who was paddling rather than pulling stroke, turned round on his young brother sharply.

" Whom do you mean ? " he asked, speaking low, so that the other occupants of the boat should not hear him, " Mary and Dowton ? "

" No," said Will, " Mary and Angus. I wonder what they see in her."

They were bound for a picnicking resort up the river; Mrs. Meredith, Mary, and Sir Clement

in the punt, and the others in the boat. If Rob
was engaged he took it gloomily. He sat in the
stern with Mr. Meredith, while Nell hid herself
away beneath a many-coloured umbrella in the
prow; and when he steered the boat into a gon-
dola, he only said vacantly to its occupants, " It is
nothing at all," as if they had run into him. Nell's
father said something about not liking the appearance of the sky, and Rob looked at him earnestly
for such a length of time before replying that Mr.
Meredith was taken aback. At times the punt
came alongside, and Mary addressed every one in
the boat except Rob. The only person in the
punt whom Rob never looked at was Mary.
Dick watched them uneasily, and noticed that
once, when Mary nearly followed her pole into the
water, Rob, who seemed to be looking in the opposite direction, was the first to see what had happened. Then Dick pulled so savagely that he
turned the boat round.

That morning at breakfast in his chambers Rob
had no thought of spending the day on the river.
He had to be at the *Wire* office at ten o'clock in
the evening, and during the day he meant to finish
one of the many articles which he still wrote for
other journals that would seldom take them. The
knowledge that Sir Clement Dowton had been to
Molesey disquieted him, chiefly because Mary
Abinger had said nothing about it. Having given

himself fifty reasons for her reticence, he pushed
them from him, and vowed wearily that he would
go to the houseboat no more.   Then Dick walked
in to suggest that they might run down for an hour
or two to Molesey, and Rob agreed at once.   He
shaped out in the train a subtle question about Sir
Clement that he intended asking Mary, but on
reaching the plank he saw her feeding the swans,
with the baronet by her side.   Rob felt like a
conjurer whose trick has not worked properly.
Giving himself just half a minute to reflect that it
was all over, he affected the coldly courteous, and
smiled in a way that was meant to be heartrending.
Mary did not mind that, but it annoyed her to see
the band of his necktie slipping over his collar.

   It was the day of the Sunbury Regatta, but the
party from the *Tawny Owl* twisted past the racers,
leaving Dick, who wanted a newspaper, behind.
When he rejoined them beyond the village, the
boat was towing the punt.

   "Why," said Dick, in some astonishment, to Rob,
who was rowing now, "I did not know you could
scull like that."

   "I have been practising a little," answered Rob.

   "When he came down here the first time," Mrs.
Meredith explained to Sir Clement, "he did not
know how to hold an oar.   I am afraid he is one of
those men who like to be best at everything."

   "He certainly knows how to scull now," admitted the baronet, beginning to think that Rob was perhaps a dangerous man. Sir Clement was a manly gentleman, but his politics were that people should not climb out of the station they were born into.

" No," Dick said, in answer to a question from Mr. Meredith, " I could only get a local paper. The woman seemed surprised at my thinking she would take in the *Scalping Knife* or the *Wire*, and said, ' We've got a paper of our own.' "

" Read out the news to us, Richard," suggested Mrs. Meredith. Dick hesitated.

" Here, Will," he said to his brother, " you got that squeaky voice of yours specially to proclaim the news from a boat to a punt ten yards distant. Angus is longing to pull us up the river unaided."

Will turned the paper round and round.

" Here is a funny thing," he bawled out, " about a stick. ' A curious story, says a London correspondent, is going the round of the clubs to-day about the walking-stick of a well-known member of Parliament, whose name I am not at liberty to mention. The story has not, so far as I am aware, yet appeared in print, and it conveys a lesson to all persons who carry walking-sticks with knobs for handles, which generate a peculiar disease in the palm of the hand. The member of Parliament referred to, with whom I am on intimate terms —' "

Rob looked at Dick, and they both groaned.

" My stick again," murmured Rob.

233

WHEN A MAN'S SINGLE

" Read something else," cried Dick, shivering.

" Eh, what is wrong ? " asked Mr. Meredith.

" You must know," said Dick, " that the first time I met Angus he told me imprudently some foolish story about a stick that bred a disease in the owner's hand, owing to his pressing so heavily on the ball it had by way of a handle. I touched the story up a little, and made half-a-guinea out of it. Since then that note has been turning up in a new dress in the most unlikely places. First the London correspondents swooped down on it, and telegraphed it all over the country as something that had happened to well-known Cabinet Ministers. It appeared in the Paris *Figaro* as a true story about Sir Gladstone, and soon afterwards it was across the channel as a reminiscence of Thiers. Having done another tour of the provinces it was taken to America by a lecturer, who exhibited the stick. Next it travelled the Continent, until it was sent home again by Paterfamilias Abroad, writing to the *Times*, who said that the man who owned the stick was a well-known Alpine guide. Since then we have heard of it fitfully as doing well in Melbourne and Arkansas. It figured in the last volume, or rather two volumes, of autobiography published, and now, you see, it is going the round of the clubs again, preparatory to starting on another tour. I wish you had kept your stick to yourself, Angus."

" That story will never die," Rob said, in a tone of conviction. " It will go round and round the world till the crack of doom. Our children's children will tell it to each other."

" Yes," said Dick, " and say it happened to a friend of theirs."

A field falls into the river above Sunbury, in which there is a clump of trees of which many boating parties know. Under the shadow of these Mrs. Meredith cast a table-cloth and pegged it down with salt-cellars.

" As we are rather in a hurry," she said to the gentlemen, " I should prefer you not to help us."

Rob wandered to the river-side with Will, who would have liked to know whether he could jump a gate without putting his hands on it; and the other men leant against the trees, wondering a little, perhaps, why ladies enjoy in the summer-time making chairs and tables of the ground.

Rob was recovering from his scare, and made friends with Mary's young brother. By particular request he not only leapt the gate, but lifted it off its hinges, and this feat of strength so impressed Will that he would have brought the whole party down to see it done. Will was as fond of Mary as a proper respect for himself would allow, but he thought she would be a lucky girl if she got a fellow who could play with a heavy gate like that.

Being a sharp boy, Will noticed a cloud settle

on Rob's face, and looking toward the clump of trees, he observed that Mary and the baronet were no longer there. In the next field two figures were disappearing, the taller, a man in a tennis jacket, carrying a pail. Sir Clement had been sent for water, and Mary had gone with him to show him the spring. Rob stared after them; and if Will could have got hold of Mary he would have shaken her for spoiling everything.

Mrs. Meredith was meditating sending some one to the spring to show them the way back, when Sir Clement and Mary again came into sight. They did not seem to be saying much, yet were so engrossed that they zigzagged toward the rest of the party like persons seeking their destination in a mist. Just as they reached the trees Mary looked up so softly at her companion that Rob turned away in an agony.

"It is a long way to the spring," were Mary's first words, as if she expected to be taken to task for their lengthened absence.

"So it seems," said Dick.

The baronet crossed with the pail to Mrs. Meredith, and stopped half-way like one waking from a dream. Mrs. Meredith held out her hand for the pail, and the baronet stammered with vexation. Simultaneously the whole party saw what was wrong, but Will only was so merciless as to put the discovery into words.

"Why," cried the boy, pausing to whistle in the middle of his sentence, "you have forgotten the water!"

It was true. The pail was empty. Sir Clement turned it upside down, and made a seat of it.

"I am so sorry," he said to Mrs. Meredith, trying to speak lightly. "I assure you I thought I had filled the pail at the spring. It is entirely my fault, for I told Miss Abinger I had done so."

Mary's face was turned from the others, so that they could not see how she took the incident. It gave them so much to think of that Will was the only one of the whole party who saw its ridiculous aspect.

"Put it down to sunstroke, Miss Meredith," the baronet said to Nell; "I shall never allow myself to be placed in a position of trust again."

"Does that mean," asked Dick, "that you object to being sent back again to the spring?"

"Ah, I forgot," said Sir Clement. "You may depend on me this time."

He seized the pail once more, glad to get away by himself to some place where he could denounce his stupidity unheard, but Mrs. Meredith would not let him go. As for Mary, she was looking so haughty now that no one would have dared to mention the pail again.

During the meal Dick felt compelled to talk so much that he was unusually dull company for the remainder of the week. The others were only genial now and again. Sir Clement sought in vain to gather from Mary's eyes that she had forgiven him for making the rest of the party couple him and her in their thoughts. Mrs. Meredith would have liked to take her daughter aside and discuss the situation, and Nell was looking covertly at Rob, who, she thought, bore it bravely. Rob had lately learned carving from a handbook, and was dissecting a fowl, murmuring to himself, "Cut from a to b along the line $f\,g$, taking care to sever the wing at the point k." Like all the others, he thought that Mary had promised to be the baronet's wife, and Nell's heart palpitated for him when she saw how gently he passed Sir Clement the mustard. Such a load lay on Rob that he felt suffocated. Nell noticed indignantly that Mary was not even "nice" to him. For the first time in her life, or at least for several weeks, Miss Meredith was wroth with Miss Abinger. Mary might have been on the rack, but she went on proudly eating bread and chicken. Relieved of his fears, Dick raged internally at Mary for treating Angus cruelly, and Nell, who had always dreaded lest things should not go as they had gone, sat sorrowfully because she had not been disappointed. They all knew how much they cared for Rob now, all except Mary of the stony heart.

Sir Clement began to tell some travellers' tales,

omitting many things that were creditable to his bravery, and Rob found himself listening with a show of interest, wondering a little at his own audacity in competing with such a candidate. By and by some members of the little party drifted away from the others, and an accident left Mary and Rob together. Mary was aimlessly plucking the berries from a twig in her hand, and all the sign she gave that she knew of Rob's presence was in not raising her head. If love is ever unselfish his was at that moment. He took a step forward, and then Mary, starting back, looked round hurriedly in the direction of Sir Clement. What Rob thought was her meaning flashed through him, and he stood still in pain.

"I am sorry you think so meanly of me," he said, and passed on. He did not see Mary's arms rise involuntarily, as if they would call him back. But even then she did not realize what Rob's thoughts were. A few yards away Rob, moving blindly, struck against Dick.

"Ah, I see Mary there," her brother said, "I want to speak to her. Why, how white you are, man!"

"Abinger," Rob answered, hoarsely, "tell me. I must know. Is she engaged to Dowton?"

Dick hesitated. He felt sore for Rob. "Yes, she is," he replied. "You remember I spoke of this to you before." Then Dick moved on to have it out with Mary. She was standing with the twig in her hand, just as Rob had left her.

"Mary," said her brother, bluntly, "this is too bad. I would have expected it from any one sooner than from you."

"What are you talking about?" asked Mary, frigidly.

"I am talking about Angus, my friend. Yes, you may smile, but it is not play to him."

"What have I done to your friend?" said Mary, looking Dick in the face.

"You have crushed the life for the time being out of as fine a fellow as I ever knew. You might at least have amused yourself with some one a little more experienced in the ways of women."

"How dare you, Dick?" exclaimed Mary, stamping her foot. All at once Dick saw that though she spoke bravely her lips were trembling. A sudden fear seized him.

"I presume that you are engaged to Dowton?" he said, quickly.

"It is presumption certainly," replied Mary.

"Why, what else could any one think after that ridiculous affair of the water?"

"I shall never forgive him for that," Mary said, flushing.

"But he —"

"No. Yes, he did, but we are not engaged."

"You mean to say that you refused him?"

"Yes."

Dick thought it over, tapping the while on a tree trunk like a woodpecker.

"Why," he asked at last.

Mary shrugged her shoulders, but said nothing.

"You seemed exceedingly friendly," said Dick, "when you returned here together."

"I suppose," Mary said, bitterly, "that the proper thing in the circumstances would have been to wound his feelings unnecessarily as much as possible?"

"Forgive me, dear," Dick said, kindly; "of course I misunderstood — but this will be a blow to our father."

Mary looked troubled.

"I could not marry him, you know, Dick," she faltered.

"Certainly not," Dick said, "if you don't care sufficiently for him; and yet he seems a man that a girl might care for."

"Oh, he is," Mary exclaimed. "He was so manly and kind that I wanted to be nice to him."

"You have evidently made up your mind, sister mine," Dick said, "to die a spinster."

"Yes," said Mary, with a white face.

Suddenly Dick took both her hands, and looked her in the face.

"Do you care for any other person, Mary?" he asked, sharply.

Mary shook her head, but she did not return her brother's gaze. Her hands were trembling. She tried to pull them from him, but he held her firmly until she looked at him. Then she drew up her head proudly. Her hands ceased to shake. She had become marble again.

Dick was not deceived. He dropped her hands, and leant despondently against a tree.

"Angus — " he began.

"You must not," Mary cried; and he stopped abruptly.

"It is worse than I could have feared," Dick said.

"No, it is not," said Mary, quickly. "It is nothing. I don't know what you mean."

"It was my fault bringing you together. I should have been more — "

"No, it was not. I met him before. Whom are you speaking about?"

"Think of our father, Mary."

"Oh, I have!"

"He is not like you. How could he dare — "

"Dick, don't."

Will bounced towards them with a hop, step, and jump, and Mrs. Meredith was signalling that she wanted both.

"Never speak of this again," Mary said in a low voice to Dick as they walked toward the others.

" I hope I shall never feel forced to do so," Dick replied.

" You will not," Mary said, in her haste. " But, Dick," she added, anxiously, " surely the others did not think what you thought? It would be so unpleasant for Sir Clement."

" Well, I can't say," Dick answered.

" At all events, he did not? "

" Who is he? "

" Oh, Dick, I mean Mr. Angus."

Dick bit his lip, and would have replied angrily; but perhaps he loved this sister of his more than any other person in the world.

" Angus, I suppose, noticed nothing," he answered, in order to save Mary pain, " except that you and Dowton seemed very good friends."

Dick knew that this was untrue. He did not remember then that the good-natured lies live for ever like the others.

Evening came on before they returned to the river, and Sunbury, now blazing with fireworks, was shooting flaming arrows at the sky. The sweep of water at the village was one broad bridge of boats, lighted by torches and Chinese lanterns of every hue. Stars broke overhead, and fell in showers. It was only possible to creep ahead by pulling in the oars and holding on to the stream of craft of all kinds that moved along by inches. Rob, who was punting Dick and Mary, had to lay down his pole and adopt the same tactics, but boat and punt were driven apart, and soon tangled hopelessly in different knots.

"It is nearly eight o'clock," Dick said, after he had given up looking for the rest of the party. "You must not lose your train, Angus."

"I thought you were to stay overnight, Mr. Angus," Mary said.

Possibly she meant that had she known he had to return to London, she would have begun to treat him better earlier in the day, but Rob thought she only wanted to be polite for the last time.

"I have to be at the *Wire*," he replied, "before ten."

Mary, who had not much patience with business, and fancied that it could always be deferred until next day if one wanted to defer it very much, said, "Oh!" and then asked, "Is there not a train that would suit from Sunbury?"

Rob, blinder now than ever, thought that she wanted to get rid of him.

"If I could catch the 8.15 here," he said, "I would reach Waterloo before half-past nine."

"What do you think?" asked Dick. "There is no time to lose."

Rob waited for Mary to speak, but she said nothing.

"I had better try it," he said.

244

With difficulty the punt was brought near a landing-stage, and Rob jumped out.

"Good-bye," he said to Mary.

"Good-night," she replied. Her mouth was quivering, but how could he know?

"Wait a moment," Dick exclaimed. "We might see him off, Mary?" Mary hesitated.

"The others might wonder what had become of us," she said.

"Oh, we need not attempt to look for them in this maze," her brother answered. "We shall only meet them again at the *Tawny Owl*."

The punt was left in charge of a boatman, and the three set off silently for the station, Mary walking between the two men. They might have been soldiers guarding a deserter.

What were Mary's feelings? She did not fully realize as yet that Rob thought she was engaged to Dowton. She fancied that he was sulky because a circumstance of which he knew nothing made her wish to treat Sir Clement with more than usual consideration; and now she thought that Rob, having brought it on himself, deserved to remain miserable until he saw that it was entirely his own fault. But she only wanted to be cruel to him now to forgive him for it afterwards.

Rob had ceased to ask himself if it was possible that she had not promised to be Dowton's wife.

His anger had passed away. Her tender heart, he thought, made her wish to be good to him — for the last time.

As for Dick, he read the thoughts of both, and inwardly called himself a villain for not reading them out aloud. Yet by his merely remaining silent these two lovers would probably never meet again, and was not that what would be best for Mary?

Rob leant out of the carriage window to say good-bye, and Dick, ill at ease, turned his back on the train. It had been a hard day for Mary, and, as Rob pressed her hand warmly, a film came over her eyes. Rob saw it, and still he thought that she was only sorry for him. There are far better and nobler things than loving a woman and getting her, but Rob wanted Mary to know, by the last look he gave her, that so long as it meant her happiness his misery was only an unusual form of joy.

CHAPTER XV

ONE misty morning, about three weeks after the picnic, Dick found himself a prisoner in the quadrangle of Frobisher's Inn. He had risen to catch an early train, but the gates were locked, and the porter in charge had vanished from his box. Dick chafed, and tore round the Inn in search of him. It was barely six o'clock ; which is three hours after midnight in London. The windows of the Inn had darkened one by one, until for hours the black building had slept heavily with only one eye open. Dick recognized the window, and saw Rob's shadow cast on its white blind. He was standing there, looking up a little uneasily, when the porter tramped into sight.

" Is Mr. Angus often as late as this ? " Mary's brother paused to ask at the gate.

" Why, sir," the porter answered, " I am on duty until eight o'clock, and as likely as not he will still be sitting there when I go. His shadow up there has become a sort of companion to me in the long nights, but I sometimes wonder what has come over the gentleman of late."

247

Dick turned away his head, to leave the rest to fate.

"So, of course I must not go," Rob continued, bravely.

Dick did not dare to look him in the face, but Rob put his hand on the shoulder of Mary's brother.

"I was a madman," he said, "to think that she could ever have cared for me, but this will not interfere with our friendship, Abinger?"

"Surely not," said Dick, taking Rob's hand.

It was one of those awful moments in men's lives when they allow, face to face, that they like each other.

Rob concluded that Mrs. Meredith, knowing nothing of his attachment for Mary, saw no reason why he should not return to the houseboat, and that circumstances had compelled Mary to write the invitation. His blundering honesty would not let him concoct a polite excuse for declining it, and Mrs. Meredith took his answer amiss, while Nell dared not say what she thought for fear of Dick. Mary read his note over once, and then went for a solitary walk round the island. Rob saw her from the tow-path, where he had been prowling about for hours in hopes of catching a last glimpse of her. Her face was shaded beneath her big straw hat, and no baby-yacht, such as the Thames sports, ever glided down the river more prettily than she tripped along the island path. Once her white frock caught in a dilapidated seat, and she had to stoop to loosen it. Rob's heart stopped beating for a moment just then. The way Mary extricated herself was another revelation. He remembered having thought it delightful that she seldom knew what day of the month it was, and having looked on in an ecstasy while she searched for the pocket of her dress. The day before Mrs. Meredith had not been able to find her pocket, and Rob had thought it foolish of ladies not to wear their pockets where they could be more easily got at.

Rob did not know it, but Mary saw him. She had but to beckon, and in three minutes he would have been across the ferry. She gave no sign, however, but sat dreamily on the ramshackle seat that patient anglers have used until the Thames fishes must think seat and angler part of the same vegetable. Though Mary would not for worlds have let him know that she saw him, she did not mind his standing afar off and looking at her. Once after that Rob started involuntarily for Molesey, but realizing what he was about by the time he reached Surbiton, he got out of the train there and returned to London.

An uneasy feeling possessed Dick that Mary knew of the misunderstanding which kept Rob away, and possibly even of her brother's share in

fostering it. If so, she was too proud to end it.
He found that if he mentioned Rob to her she did
not answer a word. Nell's verbal experiments in
the same direction met with a similar fate, and
every one was glad when the colonel reappeared to
take command.

Colonel Abinger was only in London for a few
days, being on his way to Glen Quharity, the tenant
of which was already telegraphing him glorious
figures about the grouse. Mary was going too,
and the Merediths were shortly to return to Silchester.

"There is a Thrums man on this stair," Dick
said to his father one afternoon in Frobisher's Inn,
"a particular friend of mine, though I have treated
him villainously."

"Ah," said the colonel, who had just come up
from the houseboat, "then you might have him in,
and make your difference up. Perhaps he could
give me some information about the shooting."

"Possibly," Dick said; "but we have no difference to make up, because he thinks me as honest
as himself. You have met him, I believe."

"What did you say his name was?"

"His name is Angus."

"I can't recall any Angus."

"Ah, you never knew him so well as Mary and
I do."

"Mary?" asked the colonel, looking up quickly.

"Yes," said Dick. "Do you remember a man from a Silchester paper who was at the Castle last Christmas?"

"What!" cried the colonel, "an underbred, poaching fellow who—"

"Not at all," said Dick, "an excellent gentleman, who is to make his mark here, and, as I have said, my very particular friend."

"That fellow turned up again," groaned the colonel.

"I have something more to tell you of him," continued Dick, remorselessly. "I have reason to believe, as we say on the press when hard up for copy, that he is in love with Mary."

The colonel sprang from his seat. "Be calm," said Dick.

"I am calm," cried the colonel, not saying another word, so fearful was he of what Dick might tell him next.

"That would not perhaps so much matter," Dick said, coming to rest at the back of a chair, "if it were not that Mary seems to have an equal regard for him."

Colonel Abinger's hands clutched the edge of the table, and it was not a look of love he cast at Dick.

"If this be true," he exclaimed, his voice breaking in agitation, "I shall never forgive you, Richard, never. But I don't believe it."

Dick felt sorry for his father.

"It is a fact that has to be faced," he said, more gently.

"Why, why, why, the man is a pauper!"

"Not a bit of it," said Dick. "He may be on the regular staff of the *Wire* any day now."

"You dare to look me in the face, and tell me you have encouraged this, this ——" cried the colonel, choking in a rush of words.

"Quite the contrary," Dick said; "I have done more than I had any right to do to put an end to it."

"Then it is ended?"

"I can't say."

"It shall be ended," shouted the colonel, making the table groan under his fist.

"In a manner," Dick said, "you are responsible for the whole affair. Do you remember when you were at Glen Quharity two or three years ago asking a parson called Rorrison, father of Rorrison the war correspondent, to use his son's press influence on behalf of a Thrums man? Well, Angus is that man. Is it not strange how this has come about?"

"It is enough to make me hate myself," replied the irate colonel, though it had not quite such an effect as that.

When his father had subsided a little, Dick told him of what had been happening in England during the last month or two. There had been a change

256

of Government, but the chief event was the audacity of a plebeian in casting his eyes on a patrician's daughter. What are politics when the pipes in the bath-room burst?

"So you see," Dick said in conclusion, "I have acted the part of the unrelenting parent fairly well, and I don't like it."

"Had I been in your place," replied the colonel, "I would have acted it a good deal better."

"You would have told Angus that you considered him, upon the whole, the meanest thing that crawls, and that if he came within a radius of five miles of your daughter you would have the law of him? Yes; but that sort of trespassing is not actionable nowadays; and besides, I don't know what Mary might have said."

"Trespassing!" echoed the colonel; "I could have had the law of him for trespassing nearly a year ago."

"You mean that time you caught him fishing in the Dome? I only heard of that at second-hand, but I have at least no doubt that he fished to some effect."

"He can fish," admitted the colonel; "I should like to know what flies he used."

Dick laughed.

"Angus," he said, "is a man with a natural aptitude for things. He does not, I suspect, even make love like a beginner."

"You are on his side, Richard."

"It has not seemed like it so far, but, I confess, I have certainly had enough of shuffling."

"There will be no more shuffling," said the colonel, fiercely. "I shall see this man and tell him what I think of him. As for Mary ——"

He paused.

"Yes," said Dick, "Mary is the difficulty. At present I cannot even tell you what she is thinking of it all. Mary is the one person I could never look in the face when I meditated an underhand action — I remember how that sense of honour of hers used to annoy me when I was a boy — and so I have not studied her countenance much of late."

"She shall marry Dowton," said the colonel, decisively.

"It is probably a pity, but I don't think she will," replied Dick. "Of course you can prevent her marrying Angus by simply refusing your consent."

"Yes, and I shall refuse it."

"Though it should break her heart she will never complain," said Dick, "but it does seem a little hard on Mary that we should mar her life rather than endure a disappointment ourselves."

"You don't look at it in the proper light," said the colonel, who, like most persons, made the proper light himself; "in saving her from this man we do her the greatest kindness in our power."

"Um," said Dick, "of course. That was how I put it to myself, but just consider Angus calmly, and see what case we have against him."

"He is not a gentleman," said the colonel.

"He ought not to be, according to the proper light, but he is."

"Pshaw!" the colonel exclaimed, pettishly. "He may have worked himself up into some sort of position, like other discontented men of his class, but he never had a father."

"He says he had a very good one. Weigh him, if you like, against Dowton, who is a good fellow in his way, but never, so far as I know, did an honest day's work in his life. Dowton's whole existence has been devoted to pleasure-seeking, while Angus has been climbing up ever since he was born, and with a heavy load on his back, too, most of the time. If he goes on as he is doing, he will have both a good income and a good position shortly."

"Dowton's position is made," said the colonel.

"Exactly," said Dick, "and Angus is making his for himself. Whatever other distinction we draw between them is a selfish one, and I question if it does us much credit."

"I have no doubt," said the colonel, "that Mary's pride will make her see this matter as I do."

"It will at least make her sacrifice herself for our pride, if you insist on that."

259

Mary's father loved her as he had loved her mother, though he liked to have his own way with both of them. His voice broke a little as he answered Dick.

"You have a poor opinion of your father, my boy," he said. "I think I would endure a good deal if Mary were to be the happier for it."

Dick felt a little ashamed of himself.

"Whatever I may say," he answered, "I have at least acted much as you would have done yourself. Forgive me, father."

The colonel looked up with a wan smile.

"Let us talk of your affairs rather, Richard," he said. "I have at least nothing to say against Miss Meredith."

Dick moved uncomfortably in his chair, and then stood up, thinking he heard a knock at the door.

"Are you there, Abinger?" some one called out. "I have something very extraordinary to tell you."

Dick looked at his father, and hesitated. "It is Angus," he said.

"Let him in," said the colonel.

CHAPTER XVI

Rob started when he saw Mary's father.

"We have met before, Mr. Angus," said the colonel, courteously.

"Yes," answered Rob, without a tremor; "at Dome Castle, was it not?"

This was the Angus who had once been unable to salute anybody without wondering what on earth he ought to say next. This was the colonel whose hand had gaped five minutes before for Rob's throat. The frown on the face of Mary's father was only a protest against her lover's improved appearance. Rob was no longer the hobbledehoy of last Christmas. He was rather particular about the cut of his coat. He had forgotten that he was not a colonel's social equal. In short, when he entered a room now he knew what to do with his hat. Their host saw the two men measuring each other. Dick never smiled, but sometimes his mouth twitched, as now.

"You had something special to tell me, had you not?" he asked Rob.

261

"Well," Rob replied, with hesitation, "I have something for you in my rooms."

"Suppose my father," began Dick, meaning to invite the colonel upstairs, but pausing as he saw Rob's brows contract. The colonel saw too, and resented it. No man likes to be left on the outskirts of a secret.

"Run up yourself, Abinger," Rob said, seating himself near Mary's father; "and, stop, here are my keys. I locked it in."

"Why," asked Dick, while his father also looked up, "have you some savage animal up there?"

"No," Rob said, "it is very tame."

Dick climbed the stair, after casting a quizzical look behind him, which meant that he wondered how long the colonel and Rob would last in a small room together. He unlocked the door of Rob's chambers more quickly than he opened it, for he had no notion of what might be caged up inside, and as soon as he had entered he stopped, amazed. All men of course are amazed once in their lives — when they can get a girl to look at them. This was Dick's second time.

It was the hour of the evening when another ten minutes can be stolen from the day by a readjustment of one's window curtains. Rob's blind, however, had given way in the cords, and instead of being pulled up was twisted into two triangles. Just sufficient light straggled through the window tc let Dick see the man who was standing on the hearthrug looking sullenly at his boots. There was a smell of oil in the room.

"Dowton!" Dick exclaimed; "what masquerade is this?"

The other put up his elbow, as if to ward off a blow, and then Dick opened the eyes of anger.

"Oh," he said, " it is you, is it?"

They stood looking at each other in silence.

"Just stand there, my fine fellow," Dick said, "until I light the gas. I must have a better look at you."

The stranger turned longing eyes on the door as the light struck him.

"Not a single step in that direction," said Dick, "unless you want to go over the banisters."

Abinger came closer to the man who was Sir Clement Dowton's double, and looked him over. He wore a white linen jacket, and an apron to match, and it would have been less easy to mistake him for a baronet aping the barber than it had been for the barber to ape the baronet.

"Your name?" asked Dick.

"Josephs," the other mumbled.

"You are a barber, I presume?"

"I follow the profession of hair-dressing," replied Josephs, with his first show of spirit.

Had Dick not possessed an inscrutable face, Josephs would have known that his inquisitor was suffering from a sense of the ludicrous. Dick had just remembered that his father was downstairs.

" Well, Josephs, I shall have to hand you over to the police."

" I think not," said Josephs, in his gentlemanly voice.

" Why not ? " asked Dick.

" Because then it would all come out."

" What would all come out."

" The way your father was deceived. The society papers would make a great deal of it, and he would not like that."

Dick groaned, though the other did not hear him.

" You read the society journals, Josephs ? "

" Rather ! " said Josephs.

" Perhaps you write for them ? "

Josephs did not say.

" Well, how were you brought here ? " Dick asked.

" Your friend," said Josephs, sulkily, " came into our place of business in Southampton Row half an hour ago, and saw me. He insisted on bringing me here at once in a cab. I wanted to put on a black coat, but he would not hear of it."

" Ah, then, I suppose you gave Mr. Angus the full confession of your roguery as you came along ? "

" He would not let me speak," said Josephs. " He said it was no affair of his."

THE BARBER OF ROTTEN ROW

"No? Then you will be so good as to favour me with the pretty story."

Dick lit a cigar and seated himself. The sham baronet looked undecidedly at a chair.

"Certainly not," said Dick; "you can stand."

Josephs told his tale demurely, occasionally with a gleam of humour, and sometimes with a sigh. His ambition to be a gentleman, but with no desire to know the way, had come to him one day in his youth when another gentleman flung a sixpence at him. In a moment Josephs saw what it was to belong to the upper circles. He hurried to a street corner to get his boots blacked, tossed the menial the sixpence, telling him to keep the change, and returned home in an ecstasy, penniless, but with an object in life. That object was to do it again.

At the age of eighteen Josephs slaved merrily during the week, but had never any money by Monday morning. He was a gentleman every Saturday evening. Then he lived; for the remainder of the week he was a barber. One of his delights at this period was to have his hair cut at Truefitt's, and complain that it was badly done. Having reproved his attendant in a gentlemanly way, he tipped him handsomely and retired in a glory. It was about this time that he joined a Conservative association.

Soon afterwards Josephs was to be seen in Rotten Row, in elegant apparel, hanging over the railing. He bowed and raised his hat to the ladies who took his fancy, and, though they did not respond, glowed with the sensation of being practically a man of fashion. Then he returned to the shop.

The years glided by, and Josephs discovered that he was perfectly content to remain a hairdresser if he could be a gentleman now and again. Having supped once in a fashionable restaurant, he was satisfied for a fortnight or so with a sausage and onions at home. Then the craving came back. He saved up for two months on one occasion, and then took Saturday to Monday at Cookham, where he passed as Henry K. Talbot Devereux. He was known to the waiters and boatmen there as the gentleman who had quite a pleasure in tossing them half-crowns, and for a month afterwards he had sausage without onions. So far this holiday had been the memory of his life. He studied the manners and language of the gentlemen who came to the shop in which he was employed, and began to dream of a big thing annually. He had learnt long ago that he was remarkably good-looking.

For a whole year Josephs abstained from being a gentleman except in the smallest way, for he was burning to have a handle to his name, and feared that it could not be done at less than twenty pounds. His week's holiday came, and found Josephs not ready for it. He had only twelve pounds. With a self-denial that was magnificent he crushed his aspirations, took only two days of delight at Brighton, and continued to save up for the title. Next summer saw him at the Anglers' Retreat, near Dome Castle. "Sir Clement Dow, ton" was the name on his Gladstone bag. A dozen times a day he looked at it till it frightened him, and then he tore the label off. Having done so, he put on a fresh one.

Josephs had selected his baronetcy with due care. Years previously he had been told that he looked like the twin-brother of Sir Clement Dowton, and on inquiry he had learned that the baronet was not in England. As for the Anglers' Retreat, he went there because he had heard that it was frequented by persons in the rank of life to which it was his intention to belong for the next week. He had never heard of Colonel Abinger until they met. The rest is known. Josephs dwelt on his residence at Dome Castle with his eyes shut, like a street-arab lingering lovingly over the grating of a bakery.

"Well, you are a very admirable rogue," Dick said, when Josephs had brought his story to an end, "and, though I shall never be proud again, your fluency excuses our blindness. Where did you pick it up?" The barber glowed with gratification.

"It came naturally to me," he answered. "I was intended for a gentleman. I daresay, now, I am about the only case on record of a man who took to pickles and French sauces the first time he tried them. Mushrooms were not an acquired taste with me, nor black coffee, nor caviare, nor liqueurs, and I enjoy celery with my cheese. What I liked best of all was the little round glasses you dip your fingers into when the dinner is finished. I dream of them still."

"You are burst up for the present, Josephs, I presume?"

"Yes, but I shall be able to do something in a small way next Christmas. I should like to put it off till summer, but I can't."

"There must be no more donning the name of Dowton," said Dick, trying to be stern.

"I suppose I shall have to give that up," the barber said, with a sigh. "I had to bolt, you see, last time, before I meant to go."

"Ah, you have not told me yet the why and wherefore of those sudden disappearances. Excuse my saying so, Josephs, but they were scarcely gentlemanly."

"I know it," said Josephs, sadly, "but however carefully one plans a thing, it may take a wrong turning. The first time I was at the castle I meant to leave in a carriage and pair, waving my handkerchief, but it could not be done at the money."

"The colonel would have sent you to Silchester in his own trap."

"Ah, I wanted a brougham. You see I had been a little extravagant at the inn, and I could not summon up courage to leave the castle without tipping the servants all round."

"So you waited till you were penniless, and then stole away?"

"Not quite penniless," said Josephs; "I had three pounds left, but —"

He hesitated.

"You see," he blurted out, blushing at last, "my old mother is dependent on me, and I kept the three pounds for her."

Dick took his cigar from his mouth.

"I am sorry to hear this, Josephs," he said, "because I meant to box your ears presently, and I don't know that I can do it now. How about the sudden termination to the visit you honored the colonel with last Christmas?"

"I had to go," said Josephs, "because I read that Sir Clement Dowton had returned to England. Besides, I was due at the shop."

"But you had an elegant time while your money held out?"

Josephs wiped a smile from his face.

"It was grand," he said. "I shall never know such days again."

"I hope not, Josephs. Was there no streak of cloud in those halcyon days?"

The barber sighed heavily.

"Ay, there was," he said, "hair oil."

"Explain yourself, my gentle hairdresser."

"Gentlemen," said Josephs, "don't use hair oil. I can't live without it. That is my only stumbling-block to being a gentleman."

He put his fingers through his hair, and again Dick sniffed the odor of oil.

"I had several bottles of it with me," Josephs continued, "but I dared not use it."

"This is interesting," said Dick. "I should like to know now, from you who have tried both professions, whether you prefer the gentleman to the barber."

"I do and I don't," answered Josephs. "Hair-dressing suits me best as a business, but gentility for pleasure. A fortnight of the gentleman sets me up for the year. I should not like to be a gentleman all the year round."

"The hair oil is an insurmountable obstacle."

"Yes," said the barber; "besides, to be a gentle-man is rather hard work."

"I daresay it is," said Dick, "when you take a short cut to it. Well, I presume this interview is at an end. You may go."

He jerked his foot in the direction of the door, but Josephs hesitated.

"Colonel Abinger well?" asked the barber.

"The door, Josephs," replied Dick.

"And Miss Abinger?"

Dick gave the barber a look that hurried him out of the room and down the stairs. Abinger's mouth twitched every time he took the cigar out of it, until he started to his feet.

"I have forgotten that Angus and my father are together," he murmured. "I wonder," he asked himself, as he returned to his own chambers, "how the colonel will take this? Must he be told? I think so."

Colonel Abinger was told, as soon as Rob had left, and it added so much fuel to his passion that it put the fire out.

"If the story gets abroad," he said, with a shudder, "I shall never hold up my head again."

"It is a safe secret," Dick answered; "the fellow would not dare to speak of it anywhere. He knows what that would mean for himself."

"Angus knows of it. Was it like the chivalrous soul you make him to flout this matter before us?"

"You are hard up for an argument against Angus, father. I made him promise to let me know if he ever came on the track of the impostor, and you saw how anxious he was to keep the discovery from you. He asked me at the door when he was going out not to mention it to either you or Mary."

"Confound him," cried the colonel, testily; "but he is right about Mary; we need not speak of it to her. She never liked the fellow."

"That was fortunate," said Dick, "but you did,

271

father. You thought that Josephs was a gentle-man, and you say that Angus is not. Perhaps you have made a mistake in both cases."

"I say nothing against Angus," replied the colonel, "except that I don't want him to marry my daughter."

"Oh, you and he got on well together, then?"

"He can talk. The man has improved."

"You did not talk about Mary?" asked Dick.

"We never mentioned her; how could I, when he supposes her engaged to Dowton? I shall talk about him to her, though."

Two days afterwards Dick asked his father if he had talked to Mary about Angus yet.

"No, Richard," the old man admitted, feebly, "I have not. The fact is that she is looking so proud and stately just now, that I feel nervous about broaching the subject."

"That is exactly how I feel," said Dick, "but Nell told me to-day that, despite her hauteur before us, Mary is wearing her heart away."

The colonel's fingers beat restlessly on the mantelpiece.

"I'm afraid she does care for Angus," he said.

"As much as he cares for her, I believe," replied Dick. "Just think," he added, bitterly, "that these two people love each other for the best that is in them, one of the rarest things in life, and are nevertheless to be kept apart. Look here."

Dick drew aside his blind, and pointed to a light cast on the opposite wall from a higher window.

"That is Angus's light," he said. "On such a night as this, when he is not wanted at the *Wire*, you will see that light blazing into the morning. Watch that moving shadow; it is the reflection of his arm as he sits there writing, writing, writing with nothing to write for, and only despair to face him when he stops. Is it not too bad?"

"They will forget each other in time," said the colonel. "Let Dowton have another chance. He is to be at the Lodge."

"But if they don't forget each other; if Dowton fails again, and Mary continues to eat her heart in silence, what then?"

"We shall see."

"Look here, father, I cannot play this pitiful part before Angus for ever. Let us make a bargain. Dowton gets a second chance; if he does not succeed, it is Angus's turn. Do you promise me so much?"

"I cannot say," replied the colonel, thoughtfully. "It may come to that."

Rob was as late in retiring to rest that night as Dick had predicted, but he wrote less than usual. He had something to think of as he paced his room, for, unlike her father and brother, he knew that when Mary was a romantic schoolgirl she had dressed the sham baronet, as a child may dress her doll, in the virtues of a hero. He shuddered to think of her humiliation should she ever hear the true story of Josephs — as she never did. Yet many a lady of high degree has given her heart to a baronet who was better fitted to be a barber.

CHAPTER XVII

ROB PULLS HIMSELF TOGETHER

In a London fog the street-lamps are up and about, running maliciously at pedestrians. He is in love or writing a book who is struck by one without remonstrating. One night that autumn a fog crept through London a month before it was due, and Rob met a lamp-post the following afternoon on his way home from the *Wire* office. He passed on without a word, though he was not writing a book. Something had happened that day, and, but for Mary Abinger, Rob would have been wishing that his mother could see him now.

The editor of the *Wire* had called him into a private room, in which many a young gentleman, who only wanted a chance to put the world to rights, has quaked, hat in hand, before now. It is the dusty sanctum from which Mr. Rowbotham wearily distributes glory or consternation, sometimes with niggardly hand and occasionally like an African explorer scattering largess among the natives. Mr. Rowbotham might be even a greater editor than he is if he was sure that it is quite the

proper thing for so distinguished a man as himself
to believe in anything, and some people think that
his politics are to explain away to-day the position
he took up yesterday.   He seldom writes himself,
and, while directing the line to be adopted by his
staff, he smokes a cigar which he likes to probe
with their pens.   He is pale and thin, and has rov-
ing eyes, got from always being on the alert against
aspirants.

All the chairs in the editorial room, except Mr.
Rowbotham's own, had been converted, like the
mantelpiece, into temporary bookcases.   Rob
tumbled the books off one (your "Inquiry into
the State of Ireland" was among them, gentle
reader) much as a coal-heaver topples his load
into a cellar, or like a housewife emptying her
apron.

"You suit me very well, Angus," the editor
said.   "You have no lurking desire to write a
book, have you?"

"No," Rob answered; "since I joined the Press
that ambition seems to have gone from me."

"Quite so," said Mr. Rowbotham, his tone implying that Rob now left the court without a stain
upon his character.   The editor's cigar went out,
and he made a spill of a page from "Sonnets
of the Woods," which had just come in for review.

"As you know," the editor continued, "I have
been looking about me for a leader-writer for the

last year. You have a way of keeping your head that I like, and your style is not so villainously bad. Are you prepared to join us?"

"I should think so," said Rob.

"Very well. You will start with £800 a year. Ricketts, as you may have heard, has half as much again as that, but he has been with us some time."

"All right," said Rob, calmly, though his chest was swelling. He used to receive an order for a sack of shavings in the same tone.

"You expected this, I daresay?" asked the editor.

"Scarcely," said Rob. "I thought you would offer the appointment to Marriott; he is a much cleverer man than I am."

"Yes," assented Mr. Rowbotham, more readily than Rob thought necessary. "I have had Marriott in my eye for some time, but I rather think Marriott is a genius, and so he would not do for us."

"You never had that suspicion of me?" asked Rob, a little blankly.

"Never," said the editor, frankly. "I saw from the first that you were a man to be trusted. Moderate Radicalism is our policy, and not even Ricketts can advocate moderation so vehemently as you do. You fight for it with a flail. By the way, you are Scotch, I think?"

"Yes," said Rob.

" I only asked," the editor explained, " because of the shall and the will difficulty. Have you got over that yet ? "

" No," Rob said, sadly, " and never will."

" I shall warn the proof-readers to be on the alert," Mr. Rowbotham said, laughing, though Rob did not see what at. " Dine with me at the Garrick on Wednesday week, will you ? "

Rob nodded, and was retiring, when the editor called after him —

" You are not a married man, Angus ? "

" No," said Rob, with a sickly smile.

" Ah, you should marry," recommended Mr. Rowbotham, who is a bachelor. " You would be worth another two hundred a year to us then. I wish I could find the time to do it myself."

Rob left the office a made man, but looking as if it all had happened some time ago. There were men shivering in Fleet Street as he passed down it who had come to London on the same day as himself, every one with a tragic story to tell now, and some already seeking the double death that is called drowning care. Shadows of university graduates passed him in the fog who would have been glad to carry his bag. That night a sandwich-board man, who had once had a thousand a year, crept into the Thames. Yet Rob bored his way home, feeling that it was all in vain.

He stopped at Abinger's door to tell him what

had happened, but the chambers were locked. More like a man who had lost £800 a year than one who had just been offered it, he mounted to his own rooms, hardly noticing that the door was now ajar. The blackness of night was in the sitting-room, and a smell of burning leather.

"Another pair of slippers gone," said a voice from the fireplace. It was Dick, and if he had not jumped out of one of the slippers he would have been on fire himself. Long experience had told him the exact moment to jump.

"I tried your door," Rob said. "I have news for you."

"Well," said Dick, "I forced my way in here because I have something to tell you, and resolved not to miss you. Who speaks first? My news is bad — at least for me."

"Mine is good," said Rob; "we had better finish up with it."

"Ah," Dick replied, "but when you hear mine you may not care to tell me yours."

Dick spoke first, however, and ever afterwards was glad that he had done so.

"Look here, Angus," he said, bluntly, "I don't know that Mary is engaged to Dowton."

Rob stood up and sat down again.

"Nothing is to be gained by talking in that way," he said, shortly. "She was engaged to him six weeks ago."

279

"No," said Dick, "she was not, though for all I know, she may be now."

Then Dick told his tale under the fire of Rob's eyes. When it was ended Rob rose from his chair, and stared silently for several minutes at a vase on the mantelpiece. Dick continued talking, but Rob did not hear a word.

"I can't sit here, Abinger," he said; "there is not room to think. I shall be back presently."

He was gone into the fog the next moment. "At it again," muttered the porter, as Rob swung past and was lost ten paces off. He was back in an hour, walking more slowly.

"When the colonel writes to you," he said, as he walked into his room, "does he make any mention of Dowton?"

"He never writes," Dick answered; "he only telegraphs me now and again, when a messenger from the Lodge happens to be in Thrums."

"Miss Abinger writes?"

"Yes. I know from her that Dowton is still there, but that is all."

"He would not have remained so long," said Rob, "unless — unless — "

"I don't know," Dick answered. "You see it would all depend on Mary. She had a soft heart for Dowton the day she refused him, but I am not sure how she would take his reappearance on the scene again. If she resented it, I don't think the boldest baronet that breathes would venture to propose to Mary in her shell."

" The colonel might press her ? "

" Hardly, I think, to marry a man she does not care for. No, you do him an injustice. What my father would like to have is the power to compel her to care for Dowton. No doubt he would exercise that if it was his."

" Miss Abinger says nothing — sends no messages — I mean, does she ever mention me when she writes ? "

" Never a word," said Dick. " Don't look pale, man; it is a good sign. Women go by contraries, they say. Besides, Mary is not like Mahomet. If the mountain won't go to her, she will never come to the mountain."

Rob started, and looked at his hat.

" You can't walk to Glen Quharity Lodge to-night," said Dick, following Rob's eyes.

" Do you mean that I should go at all ? "

" Why, well, you see, it is this awkward want of an income that spoils everything. Now, if you could persuade Rowbotham to give you a thousand a year, that might have its influence on my father."

" I told you," exclaimed Rob ; " no, of course I did not. I joined the staff of the *Wire* to-day at £800."

" Your hand, young man," said Dick, very nearly

becoming excited. " Then that is all right. On the Press every one with a good income can add two hundred a year to it. It is only those who need the two hundred that cannot get it."

" You think I should go north?" said Rob, with the whistle of the train already in his ears.

" Ah, it is not my affair," answered Dick; " I have done my duty. I promised to give Dowton a fair chance, and he has had it. I don't know what use he has made of it, remember. You have over-looked my share in this business, and I retire now.'

" You are against me still, Abinger."

" No, Angus, on my word I am not. You are as good a man as Dowton, and if Mary thinks you better — "

Dick shrugged his shoulders to signify that he had freed them of a load of prejudice.

" But does she ? " said Rob.

" You will have to ask herself," replied Dick.

" Yes; but when ? "

" She will probably be up in town next season."

" Next season," exclaimed Rob; " as well say next century."

" Well, if that is too long to wait, suppose you come to Dome Castle with me at Christmas ? "

Rob pushed the invitation from him contemp-tuously.

" There is no reason," he said, looking at Dick defiantly, " why I should not go north to-night."

"It would be a little hurried, would it not?"
Dick said to his pipe.

"No," Rob answered, with a happy inspiration.
"I meant to go to Thrums just now, for a few days
at any rate. Rowbotham does not need me until
Friday."

Rob looked up and saw Dick's mouth twitching.
He tried to stare Mary's brother out of countenance, but could not do it.

Night probably came on that Tuesday as usual,
for Nature is as much as man a slave to habit, but
it was not required to darken London. If all the
clocks and watches had broken their mainsprings
no one could have told whether it was at noon or
midnight that Rob left for Scotland. It would
have been equally impossible to say from his face
whether he was off to a marriage or a funeral. He
did not know himself.

"This human nature is a curious thing," thought
Dick, as he returned to his rooms. "Here are two
of us in misery, the one because he fears he is not
going to be married, and the other because he
knows he is."

He stretched himself out on two chairs.

"Neither of us, of course, is really miserable.
Angus is not, for he is in love; and I am not,
for —" He paused, and looked at his pipe.

"No, I am not miserable; how could a man be
miserable who has two chairs to lie upon, and a

tobacco jar at his elbow? I fancy, though, that I am just saved from misery by lack of sentiment.

"Curious to remember that I was once sentimental with the best of them. This is the Richard who sat up all night writing poems to Nell's eyebrows. Ah, poor Nell!

"I wonder, is it my fault that my passion burned itself out in one little crackle? With most men, if the books tell true, the first fire only goes out after the second is kindled, but I seem to have no more sticks to light.

"I am going to be married, though I would much rather remain single. My wife will be the only girl I ever loved, and I like her still more than any other girl I know. Though I shuddered just now when I thought of matrimony, there can be little doubt that we shall get on very well together.

"I should have preferred her to prove as fickle as myself, but now true she has remained to me! Not to me, for it is not the real Dick Abinger she cares for, and so I don't know that Nell's love is of the kind to make a man conceited. Is marriage a rash experiment when the woman loves the man for qualities he does not possess, and has not discovered in years of constant intercourse the little that is really lovable in him? Whatever I say to Nell is taken to mean the exact reverse of what I do mean; she reads my writings upside down, as one might say; she cries if I speak to her of anything more serious than flowers and waltzes, but she thinks me divine when I treat her like an infant.

" Is it weakness or strength that has kept me what the world would call true to Nell? Is a man necessarily a villain because love dies out of his heart, or has his reason some right to think the affair over and show him where he stands?

" Yes, Nell after all gets the worse of the bargain. She will have for a husband a man who is evidently incapable of a lasting affection for anybody. That, I suppose, means that I find myself the only really interesting person I know. Yet, I think, Richard, you would at times rather be somebody else — anybody almost would do.

" It is a little humiliating to remember that I have been lying to Angus for the last month or two — I, who always thought I had such a noble admiration for the truth. I did it very easily too, so I suppose there can be no doubt that I really am a very poor sort of creature. I wonder if it was for Mary's sake I lied, or merely because it would have been too troublesome to speak the truth? Except by fits and starts I have ceased apparently to be interested in anything. The only thing nowadays that rouses my indignation is the attempt on any one's part to draw me into an argument on any subject under the sun. Here is this Irish question; I can pump up an article in three paragraphs on it, but I don't really seem to care whether it is ever settled or not. Should we have a republic? I don't mind; it is all the same to me: but don't give me the casting vote. Is Gladstone a god? is Gladstone the devil? They say he is one or other, and I am content to let them fight it out. How long is it since I gave a thought to religion? What am I? There are men who come into this room and announce that they are agnostics, as if that were a new profession. Am I an agnostic? I think not; and if I was I would keep it to myself. My soul does not trouble me at all, except for five minutes or so now and again. On the whole I seem to be indifferent as to whether I have one, or what is to become of it."

Dick rose and paced the room, until his face gave the lie to everything he had told himself. His lips quivered and his whole body shook. He stood in an agony against the mantelpiece with his head in his hands, and emotions had possession of him compared with which the emotions of any other person described in this book were but children's fancies. By and by he became calm, and began to undress. Suddenly he remembered something. He rummaged for his keys in the pocket of the coat he had cast off, and, opening his desk, wrote on a slip of paper that he took from it, " *Scalping Knife*, Man Frightened to Get Married (humorous) ! "

" My God ! " he groaned, " I would write an article. I think, on my mother's coffin."

CHAPTER XVIII

THE AUDACITY OF ROB ANGUS

COLONEL ABINGER had allowed the other sports-
men to wander away from him, and now lay on his
back on Ben Shee, occasionally raking the glen of
Quharity through a field-glass. It was a purple
world he saw under a sky of grey and blue; with a
white thread that was the dusty road twisting round
a heavy sweep of mountain-side, and a broken
thread of silver that was the Quharity straggling
back and forward in the valley like a stream reluctant to be gone. To the naked eye they were
bare black peaks that overlooked the glen from
every side but the south. It was not the mountains,
however, but the road that interested the colonel.
By and by he was sitting up frowning, for this is
what he saw.

From the clump of trees to the north that keeps
Glen Quharity Lodge warm in winter, a man and
a lady emerged on horseback. They had not ad-
vanced a hundred yards, when the male rider
turned back as if for something he had forgotten.
The lady rode forward alone.

A pedestrian came into sight about the same time, a mile to the south of the colonel. The field-glass lost him a dozen times, but he was approaching rapidly, and he and the rider must soon meet.

The nearest habitation to Colonel Abinger was the school-house, which was some four hundred yards distant. It stands on the other side of the white road, and is approached by a straight path down which heavy carts can jolt in the summer months. Every time the old dominie goes up and down this path, his boots take part of it along with them. There is a stone in his house, close to the door, which is chipped and scarred owing to his habit of kicking it to get the mud off his boots before he goes inside. The dominie was at present sitting listlessly on the dyke that accompanies this path to the high road.

The colonel was taking no interest in the pedestrian as yet, but he sighed as he watched the lady ride slowly forward. Where the road had broken through a bump in the valley her lithe form in green stood out as sharply as a silhouette against the high ragged bank of white earth. The colonel had recognized his daughter, and his face was troubled.

During all the time they had been at the Lodge he had never mentioned Rob Angus's name to Mary, chiefly because she had not given him a chance to lose his temper. She had been more demonstrative in her love for her father than of old, and had anticipated his wants in a way that gratified him at the moment but disturbed him afterwards. In his presence she seemed quite gaily happy, but he had noticed that she liked to slip away on to the hill-side by herself, and sit there alone for hours at a time. Sir Clement Dowton was still at the Lodge, but the colonel was despondent. He knew very well that, without his consent, Mary would never give her hand to any man, but he was equally aware that there his power ended. Where she got her notions he did not know, but since she became his housekeeper she had impressed the colonel curiously. He was always finding himself taking for granted her purity to be something so fine that it behoved him to be careful. Mary affected other people in the same way. They came to know that she was a very rare person, and so in her company they became almost fine persons themselves. Thus the natural goodness of mankind asserted itself. Of late the colonel had felt Mary's presence more than ever; he believed in her so much (often to his annoyance) that she was a religion to him.

While Colonel Abinger sat in the heather, perturbed in mind, and trying to persuade himself that it was Mary's fault, the pedestrian drew near rapidly. Evidently he and the rider would meet near the school-house, and before the male rider, who had again emerged from the clump of trees, could make up on his companion.

The dominie, who did not have such a slice of the outer world as this every day, came to the end of his path to have a look at the persons who were nearing him from opposite directions. He saw that the pedestrian wore an elegant silk hat and black coat, such as were not to be got in these parts. Only the delve with which he walked suggested a man from Thrums.

The pedestrian made a remark about the weather as he hurried past the dominie. He was now so near the colonel that his face could be distinctly seen through the field-glass. The colonel winced, and turned white and red. Then the field-glass jumped quickly to the horsewoman. The pedestrian started as he came suddenly in sight of her, and at the same moment her face lit up with joy. The colonel saw it and felt a pain at his heart. The glass shook in his hand, thus bringing the dominie accidentally into view.

The dominie was now worth watching. No sooner had the pedestrian passed him than the old man crouched so as not to seem noticeable, and ran after him. When he was within ten yards of his quarry he came to rest, and the field-glass told that he was gaping. Then the dominie turned round and hurried back to the school-house, muttering as he ran:

"It's Rob Angus come home in a lum hat, and that's one o' the leddies frae the Lodge. I maun awa to Thrums wi' this. Rob Angus, Robbie Angus, michty, what a toon there'll be aboot this!"

Rob walked up to Mary Abinger, feeling that to bid her good afternoon was like saying "Thank you" in a church when the organ stops. He felt himself a saw-miller again.

The finest thing in the world is that a woman can pass through anything, and remain pure. Mary had never been put to the test, but she could have stood it. Her soul spoke in her face, and as Rob looked at her the sound of his own voice seemed a profanation. Yet Mary was not all soul. She understood, for instance, why Rob stammered so much as he took her hand, and she was glad that she had on her green habit instead of the black one.

Sir Clement Dowton rode forward smartly to make up on Miss Abinger, and saw her a hundred yards before him from the top of a bump which the road climbs. She was leaning forward in her saddle talking to a man whom he recognized at once. The baronet's first thought was to ride on, but he drew rein.

"I have had my chance and failed," he said to himself, grimly. "Why should not he have his?"

With a last look at the woman he loved, Sir

Clement turned his horse, and so rode out of Mary Abinger's life. She had not even seen him.

" Papa has been out shooting," she said to Rob, who was trying to begin, "and I am on my way to meet him. Sir Clement Dowton is with me."

She turned her head to look for the baronet, and Rob, who had been aimlessly putting his fingers through her horse's mane, started at the mention of Sir Clement's name.

" Miss Abinger," he said, " I have come here to ask you one question. I have no right to put it, but Sir Clement, he — "

" If you want to see him," said Mary, " you have just come in time. I believe he is starting for a tour of the world in a week or so."

Rob drew a heavy breath, and from that moment he liked Dowton. But he had himself to think of at present. He remembered that he had another question to ask Miss Abinger.

" It is a very long time since I saw you," he said.

" Yes," said Mary, sitting straight in her saddle, " you never came to the houseboat those last weeks. I suppose you were too busy."

" That was not what kept me away," Rob said. " You know it was not."

Mary looked behind her again.

" There was nothing else," she said; " I cannot understand what is detaining Sir Clement."

"I thought — " Rob began.

"You should not," said Mary, looking at the school-house.

"But your brother — " Rob was saying, when he paused, not wanting to incriminate Dick.

"Yes, I know," said Mary, whose intellect was very clear to-day. She knew why Rob stopped short, and there was a soft look in her eyes as they were turned upon him.

"Your brother advised me to come north," Rob said, but Mary did not answer.

"I would not have done so," he continued, "if I had known that you knew why I stayed away from the houseboat."

"I think I must ride on," Mary said.

"No," said Rob, in a voice that put it out of the question. So Mary must have thought, for she remained there. "You thought it better," he went on, huskily, "that, whatever the cause, I should not see you again."

Mary was bending her riding-whip into a bow.

"Did you not?" cried Rob, a little fiercely.

Mary shook her head.

"Then why did you do it?" he said.

"I didn't do anything," said Mary.

"In all London," said Rob, speaking at a venture, "there has not been one person for the last two months so miserable as myself."

Mary's eyes wandered from Rob's face far over

the heather. There might be tears in her eyes at any moment. The colonel was looking.

"That stream," said Rob, with a mighty effort, pointing to the distant Whunny, "twists round the hill on which we are now standing, and runs through Thrums. It turns the wheel of a saw-mill there, and in that saw-mill I was born and worked with my father for the great part of my life."

"I have seen it," said Mary, with her head turned away. "I have been in it."

"It was on the other side of the hill that my sister's child was found dead. Had she lived I might never have seen you."

"One of the gamekeepers," said Mary, "showed me the place where you found her with her foot in the water."

"I have driven a cart through this glen a hundred times," continued Rob, doggedly. "You see that wooden shed at the school-house; it was my father and I who put it up. It seems but yesterday since I carted the boards from Thrums."

"The dear boards," murmured Mary.

"Many a day my mother has walked from the saw-mill into this glen with my dinner in a basket."

"Good mother," said Mary.

"Now," said Rob, "now, when I come back here and see you, I remember what I am. I have lived for you from the moment I saw you, but however hard I might toil for you, there must always be a difference between us."

He was standing on the high bank, and their faces were very close. Mary shuddered.

"I only frighten you," cried Rob.

Mary raised her head, and, though her face was wet, she smiled. Her hand went out to him, but she noticed it and drew it back. Rob saw it too, but did not seek to take it. They were looking at each other bravely. His eyes proposed to her, while he could not say a word, and hers accepted him. On the hills men were shooting birds.

Rob knew that Mary loved him. An awe fell upon him. "What am I?" he cried, and Mary put her hand in his. "Don't, dear," she said, as his face sank on it; and he raised his head and could not speak.

The colonel sighed, and his cheeks were red. His head sank upon his hands. He was young again, and walking down an endless lane of green with a maiden by his side, and her hand was in his. They sat down by the side of a running stream. Her fair head lay on his shoulder, and she was his wife. The colonel's lips moved as if he were saying to himself words of love, and his arms went out to her who had been dead this many a year, and a tear, perhaps the last he ever shed, ran down his cheek.

"I should not," Mary said at last, "have let you talk to me like this."

Rob looked up with sudden misgiving.

" Why not ? " he cried.

" Papa," she said, " will never consent, and I — I knew that; I have known it all along."

" I am not going to give you up now," Rob said, passionately, and he looked as if he would run away with her at that moment.

" I had no right to listen to you," said Mary. " I did not mean to do so, but I — I " — her voice sank into a whisper — " I wanted to know — "

" To know that I loved you ! Ah, you have known all along."

" Yes," said Mary, " but I wanted — I wanted to hear you say so yourself."

Rob's arms went over her like a hoop.

" Rob, dear," she whispered, " you must go away, and never see me any more."

" I won't," cried Rob; " you are to be my wife. He shall not part us."

" It can never be," said Mary.

" I shall see him — I shall compel him to con-sent."

Mary shook her head.

" You don't want to marry me," Rob said, fiercely, drawing back from her. " You do not care for me. What made you say you did ? "

" I shall have to go back now," Mary said, and the softness of her voice contrasted strangely with the passion in his.

"I shall go with you," Rob answered, "and see your father."

"No, no," said Mary; "we must say good-bye here, now."

Rob turned on her with all the dourness of the Anguses in him.

"Good-bye," he said, and left her. Mary put her hand to her heart, but he was already turning back.

"Oh," she cried, "do you not see that it is so much harder to me than to you?"

"Mary, my beloved," Rob cried. She swayed in her saddle, and if he had not been there to catch her she would have fallen to the ground.

Rob heard a footstep at his side, and, looking up, saw Colonel Abinger. The old man's face was white, but there was a soft look in his eye, and he stooped to take Mary to his breast.

"No," Rob said, with his teeth close, "you can't have her. "She's mine."

"Yes," the colonel said, sadly; "she's yours."

CHAPTER XIX

THE VERDICT OF THRUMS

On a mild Saturday evening in the following May, Sandersy Riach, telegraph boy, emerged from the Thrums post-office, and, holding his head high, strutted off towards the Tenements. He had on his uniform, and several other boys flung gutters at it, to show that they were as good as he was.

"Wha's deid, Sandersy?" housewives flung open their windows to ask.

"It's no a death," Sandersy replied. "Na, na, far frae that. I daurna tell ye what it is, because it 's agin' the regalations, but it'll cause a michty wy doin' in Thrums this nicht."

"Juist whisper what it's aboot, Sandersy, my laddie."

"It canna be done, Easie; na, na. But them 'at wants to hear the noos, follow me to Tammas Haggart's."

Off Sandersy went, with some women and a dozen children at his heels, but he did not find Tammas in.

"I winna hae't lyin' aboot here," Chirsty, the

wife of Tammas, said, eyeing the telegram as something that might go off at any moment; "ye'll
better tak' it on to 'imsel. He's takkin' a dander
through the buryin' ground wi' Snecky Hobart."

Sandersy marched through the east town end at
the head of his following, and climbed the steep,
straight brae that leads to the cemetery. Tnere
he came upon the stone-breaker and the bellman
strolling from grave to grave. Silva McQuhatty
and Sam'l Todd were also in the burying ground
for pleasure, and they hobbled toward Tammas
when they saw the telegram in his hand.

"'Thomas Haggart,' the stone-breaker murmured, reading out his own name on the envelope,
"'Tenements, Thrums.'" Then he stared thoughtfully at his neighbours to see whether that could
be looked upon as news. It was his first telegram.

"Ay, ay, deary me," said Silva, mournfully.

"She's no very expliceet, do ye think?" asked
Sam'l Todd.

Snecky Hobart, however, as an official himself,
had a general notion of how affairs of state are
conducted.

"Rip her open, Tammas," he suggested. "That's
but the shell, I'm thinkin'."

"Does she open?" asked Tammas, with a grin.

He opened the telegram gingerly, and sat down
on a prostrate tombstone to consider it. Snecky's
fingers tingled to get at it.

"It begins in the same wy," the stone-breaker said, deliberately; "'Thomas Haggart, Tenements, Thrums.'"

"Ay, ay, deary me," repeated Silva.

"That means it's to you," Snecky said to Tammas.

"Next," continued Tammas, "comes 'Elizabeth Haggart, 101, Lower Fish Street, Whitechapel, London.'"

"She's a' names thegether," muttered Sam'l Todd, in a tone of remonstrance.

"She's a' richt," said Snecky, nodding to Tammas to proceed. "Elizabeth Haggart — that's wha the telegram comes frae."

"Ay, ay," said the stone-breaker, doubtfully, "but I ken no Elizabeth Haggart."

"Hoots," said Snecky; "it's your ain dochter Lisbeth."

"Keeps us a'," said Tammas, "so it is. I didna unerstan' at first; ye see we aye called her Leeby. Ay, an' that's whaur she bides in London too."

"Lads, lads," said Silva, "an' is Leeby gone? Ay, ay, we all fade as a leaf; so we do."

"What!" cried Tammas, his hand beginning to shake.

"Havers," said Snecky, "ye hinna come to the telegram proper yet, Tammas. What mair does it say?"

The stone-breaker conned over the words, and by and by his face wrinkled with excitement. He puffed his cheeks, and then let the air rush through his mouth like an escape of gas.

"It's Rob Angus," he blurted out.

"Man, man," said Silva, "an' him lookit sae strong an' snod when he was here i' the back-end o' last year."

"He's no deid," cried Tammas, "he's mairit. Listen, lads, 'The thing is true Rob Augus has married the colonel's daughter at a castle Rob Angus has married the colonel.'"

"Losh me!" said Sam'l, "I never believed he would manage't."

"Ay, but she reads queer," said Tammas. "First she says Rob's mairit the dochter, an' neist 'at he's mairit the colonel."

"Twa o' them!" cried Silva, who was now in a state to believe anything.

Snecky seized the telegram, and thought it over.

"I see what Leeby's done," he said, admiringly. "Ye're restreected to twenty words in a telegram, an' Leeby found she had said a' she had to say in fourteen words, so she's repeated hersel to get her full shilling's worth."

"Ye've hit it, Snecky," said Tammas. "It's juist what Leeby would do. She was aye a michty thrifty, shrewd crittur."

"A shilling's an awfu' siller to fling awa, though," said Sam'l.

"It's weel spent in this case," retorted Tammas,

sticking up for his own; "there hasna been sic a startler in Thrums since the English kirk steeple fell."

"Ye can see Angus's saw-mill frae here," exclaimed Silva, implying that this made the affair more wonderful than ever.

"So ye can," said Snecky, gazing at it as if it were some curiosity that had been introduced into Thrums in the night-time.

"To think," muttered Tammas, " 'at the sawmiller doon there should be mairit in a castle. It's beyond all. Oh, it's beyond, it's beyond."

"Sal, though," said Sam'l, suspiciously, "I wud like a sicht o' the castle. I mind o' readin' in a booky 'at every Englishman's hoose is his castle, so I'm thinkin' castle's but a name in the sooth for an ord'nar hoose."

"Weel a wat, ye never can trust thae foreigners," said Silva; "it's weel beknown 'at English is an awful pertentious langitch too. They slither ower their words in a hurried wy 'at l canna say I like; no, I canna say I like it."

"Will Leeby hae seen the castle?" asked Sam'l.

"Na," said Tammas; "it's a lang wy frae London; she'll juist hae heard o' the mairitch."

"It'll hae made a commotion in London, I dinna doot," said Snecky, "but, lads, it proves as the colonel man stuck to Rob."

'Ay, I hardly expected it."

"Ay, ay, Snecky, ye're richt. Rob'll hae manage't him. Weel, I will say this for Rob Angus, he was a crittur 'at was terrible fond o' gettin' his ain wy."

"The leddy had smoothed the thing ower wi' her faither," said Tammas, who was notorious for his knowledge of women; "ay, an' there was a brither, ye mind? Ane o' the servants up at the Lodge said to Kitty Wobster 'at they were to be mairit the same day, so I've nae doot they were."

"Ay," said Sam'l, pricking up his ears, "an' wha was the brither gettin'?"

"Weel, it was juist gossip, ye understan'. But I heard tell 'at the leddy had a tremendous tocher, an' 'at she was called Meredith."

"Meredith!" exclaimed Silva McQuhatty, "what queer names some o' thae English fowk has; ay, I prefer the ord'nar names mysel."

"I wonder," said Snecky, looking curiously at the others, "what Rob has in the wy o' wages?"

"That's been discuss't in every hoose in Thrums," said Sam'l, "but there's no doubt it's high, for it's a salary; ay, it's no wages."

"I dinna ken what Rob has," Silva said, "but some o' thae writers makes awfu' sums. There's the yeditor o' the *Tilliedrum Weekly Herald* noo. I canna tell his income, but I have it frae Dite Deuchars, wha kens, 'at he pays twa-an'-twenty pound o' rent for's hoose."

" Ay, but Rob's no a yeditor," said Sam'l.

" Ye're far below the mark wi' Rob's salary," said Tammas. " My ain opeenion is 'at he has a great hoose in London by this time, wi' twa or three servants, an' a lad in knickerbuckers to stan' ahent his chair and reach ower him to cut the roast beef."

" It may be so," said Snecky, who had heard of such things, " but if it is it'll irritate Rob michty no to get cuttin' the roast 'imsel. Thae Anguses aye like't to do a'thing for themsels."

"There's the poseetion to think o'," said Tammas.

" Thrums'll be a busy toon this nicht," said Sam'l, " when it hears the noos. Ay, I maun awa' an' tell the wife."

Having said this, Sam'l sat down on the tomb-stone.

" It'll send mair laddies on to the papers oot o' Thrums," said Tammas. " There's three awa' to the printin' trade since Rob was here, an' Susie Byars is to send little Joey to the business as sune as he's auld eneuch."

" Joey'll do weel in the noospaper line," said Silva; " he writes a better han' than Rob Angus already."

" Weel, weel, that's the main thing, lads."

Sam'l moved off slowly to take the news into the east town end.

" It's to Rob's creedit," said Tammas to the two men remaining, " 'at he was na at all prood when he came back. Ay, he called on me very frank like, as ye'll mind, an' I wasna in, so Chirsty dusts a chair for 'im, and comes to look for me. Lads, I was fair ashamed to see 'at in her fluster she'd gien him a common chair, when there was hair-bottomed anes in the other room. Ye may be sure I sent her for a better chair, an' got him to change, though he was sort o' mad like at havin' to shift. That was his ind'pendence again."

"I was aye callin' him Rob," said Snecky, "forgettin' what a grand man he was noo, an', of coorse, I corrected mysel, and said Mr. Angus. Weel, when I'd dune that mebbe a dozen times he was fair stampin's feet wi' rage, as ye micht say. Ay, there was a want o' patience aboot Rob Angus."

"He slippit a gold sovereign into my hand," said Silva, "but, losh, he wudna lat me thank 'im. 'Hold yer tongue,' he says, or words to that effec, when I insistit on't."

At the foot of the burying-ground road Sam'l Todd could be seen laying it off about Rob to a little crowd of men and women. Snecky looked at them till he could look no longer.

"I maun awa wi' the noos to the wast toon end," he said, and by and by he went, climbing the dyke for a short cut.

"Weel, weel, Rob Angus is mairit," said Silva to Tammas.

" So he is, Silva," said the stone-breaker.

" It's an experiment," said Silva.

" Ye may say so, but Rob was aye venturesome."

" Ye saw the leddy, Tammas ? "

" Ay, man, I did mair than that. She spoke to me, an' speired a lot aboot the wy Rob took on when little Davy was fund deid. He was fond o' his fowk, Rob, michty fond."

" What was your opeenion o' her then, Tammas ? "

" Weel, Silva, to tell the truth I was oncommon favourably impreesed. She shook hands wi' me, man, an' she had sic a saft voice an' sic a bonny face I was a kind o' carried awa; yes, I was so."

" Ay, ye say that, Tammas. Weel, I think I'll be movin'. They'll be keen to hear aboot this in the square."

" I said to her," continued Tammas, peering through his half-closed eyes at Silva, " 'at Rob was a lucky crittur to get sic a bonny wife."

" Ye did !" cried Silva. " An' hoo did she tak' that ? "

" Ou," said Tammas, complacently, " she took it weel."

" I wonder," said Silva, now a dozen yards away, " 'at Rob never sent ony o' the papers he writes to Thrums juist to lat's see them."

" He sent a heap," said Tammas, " to the minister, meanin' them to be passed roond, but Mr.

Dishart didna juist think they were quite the thing ye unerstan', so he keeps them lockit up in a press."

"They say in the toon," said Silva, "'at Rob would never hae got on sae weel if Mr. Dishart hadna helpit him. Do you think there's onything in that?"

Tammas was sunk in reverie, and Silva at last departed. He was out of sight by the time the stone-breaker came to.

"I spoke to the minister aboot it," Tammas answered, under the impression that Silva was still there, "an' speired at him if he had sent a line aboot Rob to the London yeditors, but he wudna say."

Tammas moved his head round, and saw that he was alone.

"No," he continued, thoughtfully, addressing the tombstones, "he would neither say 'at he did nor 'at he didna. He juist waved his han' like, to lat's see 'at he was at the bottom o't, but didna want it to be spoken o'. Ay, ay."

Tammas hobbled thoughtfully down one of the steep burying-ground walks, until he came to a piece of sward with no tombstone at its head.

"Ay," he said, "there's many an Angus lies buried there, an' Rob's the only ane left noo. I hae helpit to hap the earth ower five, ay, sax o' them. It's no to be expeckit, no, i' the course o'